SAY NO TO THE BRO

Also by Kat Helgeson

Gena/Finn

KAT HELGESON

SIMON & SCHUSTER BFYR
NEW YORK LONDON TORONTO SYDNEY NEW DELHI

SIMON & SCHUSTER BFYR
An imprint of Simon & Schuster Children's Publishing Division
1230 Avenue of the Americas, New York, New York 10020

Also available in a SIMON & SCHUSTER BFYR hardcover edition
Cover design by Krista Vossen
Interior design by Hilary Zarycky
The text for this book was set in Adobe Garamond Pro.
Manufactured in the United States of America
First SIMON & SCHUSTER BFYR paperback edition May 2018
2 4 6 8 10 9 7 5 3 1
The Library of Congress has cataloged the hardcover edition as follows:
Names: Helgeson, Kat.
Title: Say no to the bro / Kat Helgeson.
Description: First edition. | New York : SSBFYR, [2017] | Summary: "Two teens become entangled in a cut-throat prom date auction in this story that is equal parts dark comedy, high school romance, and timely social commentary; and loosely inspired by true events"—Provided by publisher.
Identifiers: LCCN 2016028164| ISBN 9781481471930 (hc)
| ISBN 9781481471954 (eBook)
Subjects: | CYAC: High schools—Fiction. | Schools—Fiction. | Proms—Fiction. |
Dating (Social customs)—Fiction. | Love—Fiction. |
BISAC: JUVENILE FICTION / Social Issues / Peer Pressure. | JUVENILE FICTION / Social Issues / Dating & Sex. | JUVENILE FICTION / Love & Romance.
Classification: LCC PZ7.1.H446 Say 2017 | DDC [Fic]—dc23
LC record available at https://lccn.loc.gov/2016028164
ISBN 9781481471947 (pbk)

For Mom & Dad–
thanks for always listening

SAY NO TO THE BRO

1

Ava

The first thing I thought when my mother left was that now I was going to have to take over the cooking.

I remember standing in the driveway of our old house in Carbondale—old in every sense of the word, built in 1903 and now a relic of the life all four of us have left behind. I was wearing a pale yellow dress that flapped around my knees as the car that wasn't Dad's sped away with my mom in the passenger seat. I'd been shopping with her just two weeks ago for that dress and it was my first time wearing it, with my hair down and sans product, the way I knew she liked it best. I wanted to make her happy. I thought maybe if she saw me in the dress, a miracle would happen. Maybe she wouldn't go.

At fifteen, there was no excuse for believing in miracles.

As the car pulled out of sight, I'd noticed the bite of the gravel against my bare feet and thought, *I'd better learn some recipes*. I'd changed into jeans and hung the dress in the back of my closet where I wouldn't have to look at it. I'd gone online and ordered a book called *Teens Cook*, which looked fun and not too complicated.

I was being proactive, and I was proud of myself. I could do this. I could be the woman of the house.

But Dad surprised me. Dad is actually a decent cook.

It's game night tonight, so we're having his signature dish—spicy chili with extra onions. My mom used to complain about the onions every time, even though Dad, Sean, and I all love them. She wouldn't have allowed devices at the table either, but Dad does, probably so he can review plays for tonight's game. Patterson High has its season opener against Mount Pleasant, and Dad needs to start the year with a win.

Honestly, I could use a win too.

Dad looks up from his phone. "Sean? Go get dressed."

My brother, who's been shoveling down chili too fast to taste it, drops his spoon with a clatter. "Why do I have to dress out? There's no JV game."

"Didn't your coach tell you to?"

"He said it was optional."

"And I say it's not. Part of being on a team is showing your support even when you're not playing."

"Dad . . ."

Dad folds his arms across his barrel chest. "Why don't you want to?"

And Sean is stumped. I knew it. He doesn't have a reason, he's just doing that fourteen-year-old obstinate thing. I've seen him in his room, brushing imaginary lint off his jersey, spit-polishing the big white number seventy-seven until there isn't a speck of dirt on it. Watching him shuffle off to get changed, I kind of wish I had my own jersey to wear to the game tonight so I could stand behind the bench and cheer Dad on the way Sean can.

"Are you coming to the game, Ava?" Dad scoops a titanic amount of chili into his mouth. A little bit dribbles down his chin. "I bet all your new friends will be there."

New friends. *Right.* Dad's fishing. I know it, and he knows I know it. He wants to hear that I'm thrilled with Patterson, that I'm part of a big crowd of kids and we're going to meet up at the game. "Maybe."

"Yeah?" Dad looks encouraged, and I can't help softening. He wants me to do well. This new coaching job means so much to him. He's been talking about his playing days at Patterson since before I can remember. There are pictures of me as a baby wrapped up in a Patterson jersey, for God's sake.

"Do you need a ride?" Dad asks, getting up to clear his plate.

"It's okay." If I ride in with Dad, he'll be looking up into the stands all through warm-ups, waiting for my alleged friends to arrive. If I go on my own, I'll be able to disappear into the crowd. I'll call Charlotte for a ride. My cousin may not count as a friend, but she's made a point of talking to me every day this week. Charlotte and I haven't spent time around each other since we were little kids, so I'm thinking maybe her mom told her to look out for me and Sean in school or something. And I know she's going, because she and her friend Elise were gossiping about the players all through Pre-Calc.

"Sean!" Dad bellows up the stairs.

"Two minutes!"

"No minutes! Now!" He turns to me. "Get him out the door, will you?"

"Okay, Dad."

Dad goes out to the car. A minute later, Sean comes thundering down the stairs. He's changed his pants and added an extra glob of gel to his shellacked hair. If I were a different kind of sister, I'd have the personal grooming talk with Sean. But the extent of my hair knowledge involves wetting it down before winding it into my customary two braids so loose ends don't poke out the sides.

Sean pauses to grab a Gatorade out of the fridge. "Coming, Ave?"

"Later."

"Dad's really charged about all this, huh?"

"Yeah, seems like."

"I mean, like . . . he's like *before*. You know. Before Mom split."

He's right, but I don't want to talk about her. "Sean, go get in the car. You're gonna make Dad late."

Sean rolls his eyes and leaves, and I'm alone in the cherrywood kitchen with high granite countertops that's too fancy and doesn't feel like it's ours yet. The wood floors are varnished and shiny, and the rag rug I made in Girl Scouts in the fourth grade is in the upstairs hallway instead of in front of the sink where it always used to be.

I think my mom would probably love this kitchen. She likes new things.

Charlotte picks me up an hour later. An hour *fashionably* later, I guess. Her hair is curled and her nails are still wet. At intervals, she lifts her hand from the steering wheel to blow on them.

"Should I have dressed up?" I know the answer to that. It's a football game, for God's sake. How many of them have I been to? It's got to be in the thousands. But maybe Patterson kids are different. Maybe they dress up for football.

Charlotte says, "Nah."

"You look good."

"Oh yeah, do you like this necklace? It's my mom's."

Charlotte's mom, my Aunt Claire, is ten years younger than Dad. She is pregnant in her wedding pictures, which Dad always shakes his head at, but she's also still happily married. Plus she apparently has great accessories. "Yeah," I tell Charlotte. "I love bronze."

"It's not *bronze*, it's rose gold!"

"You're wearing gold to the game?"

"There are going to be guys there, Ava." She glances at me, side-eye. "But don't worry. Guys are stupid about jewelry. They can't tell if something's cheap."

Surreptitiously, I slide my Forever 21 bangles off and drop them in the passenger door pocket.

"I'm so glad you decided to come out!" Charlotte takes her eyes off the road to flash me a grin.

"You are?"

"Ava, it's going to be great. I've always wanted a little sister."

"Um. Thank you."

"It'll be like having a built-in best friend, don't you think?"

"Sure, Char."

She wrinkles her nose. "Do *not* call me that. I hate nicknames."

"Oh. Sorry."

"I guess you wouldn't understand because your name kind of already is a nickname." Charlotte pulls into the parking lot and I wonder what she thinks "Ava" is short for. Avery? Avagail?

Patterson has one of the nicest football stadiums I've seen at a high school, with state-of-the-art scoreboards and seating on all four sides of the field. The marching band is high-stepping across the AstroTurf as Charlotte and I take our seats.

"Look." Charlotte grabs my arm and points. "Okay, that's Laura Baretta. She's head cheerleader."

"Oh. Are you friends?"

"Yeah, kind of," Charlotte says, with the airy no-big-deal tone of someone who could not possibly think it was a bigger deal. "I could have gotten onto the squad, but cheerleading's a little passé, at least around here. I don't know what it's like in Carterdale."

"Carbondale."

"Right."

"My dad wanted me to be a cheerleader," I confess.

"Really? Your dad? Why?"

"Because they're involved with the team, I guess."

"Why didn't you try out?"

"Come on, Charlotte."

"What?"

"You know they wouldn't have taken me."

She's quiet for a minute. "Ava, you're not . . ."

I scuff my sneaker on the bleacher.

"You're pretty." She ducks her head to look me in the eyes. "A lot of people would kill for your hair."

It's my mom's hair: big, bushy, unruly. The only thing it has in common with Dad's and Sean's is the color—auburn, where my mom's was jet-black. I don't want her hair to be the thing that makes me pretty. I wish Charlotte had mentioned my eyes, which are too big for my face and blue like Sean's, or the stupid dimple in my chin that I actually like because it comes from Dad, or even my figure, even though that would have been a transparent lie because not one of the perky girls bouncing on the sidelines is over one hundred twenty pounds or wears a bra larger than a B cup.

"I'm too big," I say to Charlotte.

She puts an arm around me. "You're not that much bigger than me."

She's lying, obviously. Charlotte has the Vanguard genes I've always wanted, the tall, slim frame topped off with feather-soft hair. She looks more like my brother than I do, and she's probably thirty pounds lighter than I am. Still, it's the thought that counts, right? "Thank you, Char."

"Charlotte."

"Right."

"Oh look! Here come the guys!"

Most football teams I've seen, when they take the field, have some kind of ritual to pump themselves up. They knock their helmets together, or they burst through a hand-painted sign made by the cheerleaders or the booster club. The Patterson team trots out like regimented soldiers. Dad's really taking this seriously.

"That's Cody Spencer," Charlotte says. "He's, like, the king of detention."

"Really? What does he do?"

"Mostly talks back to teachers. But he always brings donuts when he gets detention, so everyone likes him. And that's Brad Lennox. I totally want to go out with him this year."

"The kicker?"

"The which?"

"The one by the cooler."

"Oh. Yeah. Don't you think he's the cutest?"

"He's pretty cute, I guess." I've been watching high school football teams since I was four years old, so I've never thought of the players as potential dates. "Who's the QB?"

"That stands for quarterback, right?"

"Yeah."

"Mark Palmer." She points him out. "I hear he's pretty good."

"You hear? Don't you usually come to the football games?"

She gives me a look like I'm crazy. "Not, like, to *watch* them."

"Right." What was I thinking? "He is good. I saw them practicing during preseason."

"Hmm." She stands and waves, and two girls I don't know come over and join us. Charlotte launches into a conversation with them without even introducing me.

Seems like disappearing into the crowd is going to be easier than I thought.

Mark

My head itches from sweating into my helmet. One of my thigh pads is twisted at an awkward angle from when I landed hard, and I haven't fixed it because there's no way to do that without literally reaching down my pants. My cleats, last year's, are worn at the soles and don't absorb shock well, so my ankles kind of hurt. But who cares about any of that? We won!

Cody takes a knee in the huddle beside me. He's all out of breath, which is stupid because the long snapper isn't even involved in most plays, and when he is, he's not exactly sprinting downfield. My guess is he just came running over from the kick line that the cheerleaders have going.

"What a game!" he crows. "We killed them!"

I can't help grinning.

"Settle down, boys," says Coach Vanguard.

I think tonight proves Coach Vanguard is a more effective coach than Coach Weir was. Our summer practices were grueling as hell, so it's nice to see that pay off. And I'm going to lead us this year. Things couldn't be going better.

I know not everything was perfect tonight—the pass Deon dropped in the third quarter was mostly my fault, and I got sacked twice in the first half—but Coach won't bring up those things until practice tomorrow. Tonight he's congratulating us, pointing out who's done well and the things the whole team is doing right. I should be paying more attention, but this stuff isn't that important and I'm happy and tired and the JV kids are squirting each other with Gatorade. It's hard to focus.

One of the freshmen aims his Gatorade bottle at a girl standing behind the bench. After a beat, I recognize them. The boy is Sean Vanguard, Coach's son and a strong fullback for the JV line. He'll probably play Varsity next year. The girl has been around a few times over the summer, usually to pick Sean up from practices. I think she might be his big sister. She's got the same stance as Coach, one elbow awkwardly propped on the arm she's wrapped around her waist, chin in her hand. She doesn't look much like him though. She doesn't look much like anyone. Huge eyes. Huge hair. Huge . . . anyway.

Cody elbows me in the ribs and jerks his head toward Coach. "Dude."

Right. That'd be a fine conversation. *Why weren't you paying attention to my postgame talk, Palmer?* Oh, I was checking out your daughter, sir. *Benched forever.*

And I can't get benched. Especially not this year.

Coach finishes up his talk and tells us to hit the showers. It's a figure of speech. We do have showers in the locker room, but no one's going to hit them when we can just go home and shower there, in private. Institutional showers are probably the only part of football I don't love. I mean, I'll do it if it's early morning practice and I have classes to get to. But I won't like it.

The team begins to disperse. The unified block of purple and gold uniforms is now peppering its way throughout the bleachers as people find their parents or girlfriends. It seems everyone has someone in the crowd supporting them tonight. My parents are here too, Dad in his Patterson sweater and Mom with the crepe booster club pom-poms she's had since my freshman year. They never miss a game. They'd come to practices if I'd let them. I should go up to meet them by the bleachers, but Dad's talking to a man in a suit who I don't recognize. I know what that means, and I am so not in the mood.

The girl is still standing by the bench, alone now that the JV kids have gone to the locker room to pick up towels and water bottles. I do a quick perimeter check for Coach and don't see him anywhere. Who am I to pass up a perfect opportunity? Besides, she looks like she could use someone to talk to. "Hey."

She startles like a bird, like she didn't notice me walking over. "Me?"

"Yeah. You're new to Patterson, right?"

"Oh. Yes."

"How are you liking it?"

"Pretty good." She fidgets, hands in the pockets of her hoodie, rocking from one foot to the other. She doesn't make eye contact. This isn't a girl who's had a *pretty good* week. This girl is spooked as hell.

"So . . ." I fish for something to say. The silence is dragging and she isn't helping. "Coach Vanguard is your dad, right?"

"Did he . . . he mentioned me?"

"No, I saw you picking up Sean a few times."

"Oh." She sounds strangely disappointed. Could she really have been hoping Coach had talked about her? The last thing I'd want is to find out my parents had been talking about me to my classmates.

"You're the quarterback," she says, finally making eye contact. "Right?"

"Yeah, I am."

"Nice arm."

"You think?"

"You threw a sixty-yard pass in the second quarter."

It was sixty-five, actually, and short of my personal best, but I don't have the hubris to say so. "I have good receivers on the field."

"But a good QB, that's everything." She's animated now. "My dad always wanted a good QB. He used to say that if he could just get someone who could place a ball where it needed to go, he could drive a team all the way to a championship."

"God, I'd love a championship."

"Right? Us too."

I grin at her and she bites her lip and smiles, just a little.

"So, Sean's Sister—"

"Ava."

"Mark Palmer. Are you a senior too?"

"Yeah, I am."

"Do you know where you're going for college?"

She raises her eyebrows. "Do you really want to play that game?"

"What game?"

"You know. The twenty questions everyone asks about life after graduation. Where are you going for college? Do you have a major picked out?"

"Have you applied yet?"

"Have you been accepted?"

"Will you be working?"

"Will you have a car?"

"Are you still going to play ball?"

"Well." She giggles. "I don't get that one so much."

"So what *do* you do? Any sports? Music? Theater?"

She starts to answer, but a voice cuts her off. "Hey *Palmer*!"

I turn. Cody's slipped out of his shoulderpads so his jersey hangs loosely, like a large T-shirt. He's also in street pants. "Go change," he calls as he covers the last few feet between us. "Caity Pierce is having a postgame thing."

I look back at Ava. "Do you want to come to a party? It'll just be a lot of seniors hanging out, no stress. Caity's got a pool table."

"It's invite-only," Cody says.

"She didn't invite me," I argue.

Cody rolls his eyes. "You're the quarterback, dude. We're the Varsity football team. Don't be stupid."

Ava's backing away now. "I need to get back to my dad. He'll be worried."

"No problem. Maybe I'll see you around school?"

"Yeah. Totally. See you." And she's off, dodging into the crowd as skillfully as an assassin, gone before I can track where she went.

"Dude," says Cody.

"What?"

"Dude."

"Dude, *what*?"

"Dude, Wild Card."

"No, man, come on. She's new."

"So?"

"So leave her out of it."

He folds his arms. "You *like* her." It's an indictment. Cody is out with different girls every weekend, but he'd never stoop to *liking* one of them. Especially a girl like Ava, a clear loner with no circle of gossipy friends for Cody to work his way through.

Anyway, it's irrelevant. "I don't *like* her. I'm just trying to be a decent guy. She shouldn't have to go through the whole Prom Bowl thing on top of being the new kid."

Cody rolls his eyes. "Sure, Mark. Whatever."

"Just pick a different Wild Card, okay?"

"Whatever you say."

"I'm serious, Cody."

"Are you coming to Caity's or not?"

"I have History homework."

I don't have History homework. Cody probably knows it, too, since we have the same History teacher. I just don't want to spend all night dodging Amy Spicoli and watching my teammates chug beers.

I find Mom and Dad in the parking lot doing jigsaw puzzles on their phones. "Hey guys."

Mom jumps up. "Mark, that was wonderful! You were wonderful!"

"Thanks Mom." She's so over-the-top sometimes.

"A couple of errors," Dad says casually. "Nothing too major. Nothing that would be considered a deal breaker."

I knew it. "What scouts did you talk to?"

"Arizona. Stanford."

"Notre Dame?" Mom chimes in.

"No Notre Dame yet."

I toe off my cleats and stretch out flat on my back in the backseat. "I'm not going to Notre Dame, Mom."

"Mark, it's such a good school, you should at least—"

"It doesn't matter what college you go to," I interrupt. This fact has been drilled in by Dr. Cruz, our school guidance counselor and a close personal friend of Mom's, who we've met with countless times to discuss my future.

"Mark, that's an excuse for students who can't get into top schools. You *can*."

"It's not an excuse. What matters is that you pick a place that's right for you and work hard."

"Dr. Cruz didn't mean you shouldn't pursue big opportunities," Mom counters.

"Dr. Cruz meant I should focus on what I'm doing right now. Kicking ass—kicking *butt*, sorry Mom—on the field and in the classroom. Which is what got us here in the first place, remember?" God knows I've worked hard the past three years. I'm a student-athlete. I've gotten more scholarship offers than anyone else on the team. You'd think they could relax now, enjoy the fact that I'm going to be the first person in our family to attend college, and let me play some damn ball.

Dad seems to be thinking along the same lines. "Let's not do this tonight."

"He needs to stay focused on scholarships," Mom says like I'm not there.

"Not tonight. He just won a game. Let this go."

Thank you, Dad.

It's true that I need a scholarship or the college thing isn't going to happen, and I know I need to keep the burners on this year to prove I'm not a slacker. But I'm *not* a slacker. I'm sure the scouts saw my hustle. God, I hate this. This is why Coach doesn't give us notes until the next day. I should be able to enjoy the feeling of a victory without picking every little thing apart.

Football used to be fun, is the thing.

Now I'm just wondering whether the scout from Stanford noticed my long bomb, the one Ava mentioned.

At least I know *somebody* liked my game.

PATTERSON HIGH PROM BOWL

Private

Cody Spencer

Posted 10 min ago

Attention, Ladies!

Congratulations! YOU have been nominated by your classmates to be contestants in this year's Prom Bowl. Today there are fifteen of you. Soon, only one will remain—the PROM QUEEN.

Our first event will take place on the evening of the homecoming game and dance. Details to follow. The ten girls who receive the highest bids will progress to the next round of competition. As for the rest of you—well, just remember that all the money raised by the Prom Bowl goes toward paying for our prom, so if you get bought by Andy Mercer, hey, at least it's for a good cause!

Good luck, ladies, and remember—you can hide almost any flaw with a short skirt!

Like • Reply

Joanna York, Amy Spicoli, and 12 others like this

Marlee Wheeler

Can I raid your shoe closet **Charlotte Ramsey?**

Posted 2 min ago • **Like • Reply**

Charlotte Ramsey

Nice try, bitch. You're not winning with my heels! LOL :) <3 u!

Posted 1 min ago • **Like • Reply**

MEMBERS

Cody Spencer
Mark Palmer
Caity Pierce
Amy Spicoli
Marlee Wheeler
Solstice Downing
Emily Hickman
Denise Mellibosky
Maria Baker
Sarah Leavett
Charlotte Ramsey
Olivia Merchant
Hannah Bauman
Kylie Richards
Elizabeth Kepler
Joanna York
Wild Card: Ava Vanguard

2

Ava

At Carbondale High School, we had full desks that you could actually put your books in, but the seating in the Patterson classrooms is in the form of those chairs with the half-desk attached. Still, the basic rule of thumb is the same here as it is anywhere: to blend in, follow the leader. I let Charlotte sit down first and watch how she slouches so her butt is at the edge of the seat and her shoulders are pressed against the backrest. She looks bored and sort of daydreamy, like maybe *technically* she's here for English Lit, but no one should make the mistake of thinking she cares about Chaucer or anything. I copy her halfway-to-naptime posture and pull out my Xeroxed pages of *The Summoner's Tale*, a handout from Friday afternoon that hasn't actually been assigned to us yet.

"Are you reading that?" Charlotte asks.

In fact I am not reading it; I'm using it to avoid talking to people. The five minutes before class starts are prime time for asking the new girl questions. I know what Dad would say—*Put it down, Ava, make some friends, make yourself approachable*—but one year of solitude never killed anyone. I'll be starting over again next year anyway. I see no reason to pretend this year is anything more than an unpleasant interval I'll forget as soon as I move on. These kids are not going to be long-term characters in my life.

Well, Charlotte, maybe.

"I'm trying to read it," I tell her. Oh damn, that probably sounded like I was snapping at her for interrupting me. Why don't I ever think before I speak?

If Charlotte is offended, though, she doesn't show it. "Is it good?"

"Mostly Old English bathroom humor."

She rolls her eyes. "Gross. Hey, did I tell you Brad kissed me?"

Ah, her real reason for talking to me. "No. When?"

"Caity's party, after the game on Friday." She frowns. "I tried to find you. Where'd you disappear to?"

"Went home with my dad. Sorry, I should have told you."

"But your dad was still there when I left. I asked Sean where you were and he didn't know either."

"Oh. I was just . . . I was talking to someone."

"To who?"

"Whom." God, shut up, Ava. "Just some guy."

"Ooh, was he cute? Do you like him? Do you think he's gonna ask you out? Who was it?"

"Nobody. No, he's not going to ask me out. We were just talking."

"He could totally ask you out."

I almost have to laugh. I've been watching football players and their girlfriends as long as I can remember. I used to pretend my Barbie and Ken dolls were a placekicker named Danny and his girlfriend, Danielle. I know what the girlfriends of football players are like. They're skinny and flirty with sleek hair and short skirts, high heels and no curfews. Football players don't date girls who would rather stay home and watch *The Matrix* for the seventeenth time than go to Caity Pierce's party. Mark was just being nice to the new girl, or possibly sucking up to the coach's daughter. If I told Charlotte I'd been talking to him, she'd laugh.

The tinny chorus of a pop song echoes from the depths of Charlotte's bag. She reaches in to dig for her phone, and I turn my attention back to Chaucer. Or rather, I try, but for some reason all I can think about now is Mark and how, for the first time since we moved to Minnesota, talking to a new person didn't make me feel awkward or self-conscious. It was just easy, the way talking to my lifelong friends in Carbondale used to be.

Someone else's phone buzzes, and I automatically reach into my pocket before remembering that I left my phone in my locker. Then I hear another buzz and another ringtone, and suddenly phones are going off all around the room. What the hell?

I read a book a few months ago, a sinister and frightening story of war and terror that opened with a violent attack, which prompted everyone's parents to call them during school hours. Suddenly I'm wishing I had my phone. What if something terrible happened? What if Dad's trying to reach me and he can't? What if Sean needs me? What if—

Charlotte grabs my arm. "Ava."

"What is it? What's going on?"

"We made it."

"We made what?" My heart is pounding. "Charlotte, what's happening?"

"We *both* made it. We're in the Prom Bowl. Oh my God, Ava, you're in the Prom Bowl!"

"The what?"

Charlotte shoves her phone into my hands and bolts out of her seat to hug a blonde girl a few rows back. A numb relief washes over me. I'm looking at a Facebook page. There's no way a terrorist attack has its own Facebook page. Everything's okay.

Then I read it.

Fifteen girls have been chosen, and I am number fifteen. I have no idea whether we're ranked according to anything specific, but my name is the only one with a label on it—"Wild Card." There's going to be an "event" homecoming night. We'll be competing for bids. The winner will be named prom queen. . . .

Competing for bids?

"Charlotte?" My voice comes out sounding like a parakeet.

"Ava, come over here!"

But I can't. I'm frozen in my chair. People are bowed over their phones, whispering to their neighbors and then glancing up at me. I want to drop Charlotte's phone and run. If I get out of this chair, that's what's going to happen. I wrap my ankles around the cold metal legs and force myself to stay.

"Ava?" Charlotte's looking over my shoulder now. Her breath is hot on my cheek. I want to duck away, but I don't know how to do that without seeming rude.

I hold up the phone. "What is this?"

"Prom Bowl!"

"But what *is* it? It says people bid on us?"

"Yeah, as prom dates. It's a tradition."

"Buying prom dates is a tradition?"

"It's an honor, Ava. Everyone knows only the cutest girls get picked to compete. The girls that guys will bid the most for. It means guys would pay more for us than anyone else in our grade."

"I don't want to be paid for!"

"Well, you're already on the list. I don't think they can change it now. Everyone's voted and everything."

"Everyone *voted*? When! I didn't vote on this!"

Charlotte widens her eyes. "Okay, you need to calm down. Everyone is staring at you."

I look up. Shit. She's right. Shit shit shit. I have to get out of here.

"All right, class. Phones away, please, before I take them away." Ms. Hess bustles in and drops a pile of books on her desk. "Please take out *The Summoner's Tale* and read the first ten pages."

The chaos fades to a disgruntled murmur, and then to the quiet turning of pages. I can still feel the occasional glance flicking my way, no doubt wondering who the new girl is and how she made it onto a list of the fifteen most desirable girls in school when she is so clearly not up to par. Is it some kind of prank? What does "Wild Card" mean, and why am I the only one with the label? I huddle behind my Chaucer and focus on breathing deeply, not allowing myself the luxury of tears.

There's a way out of this. There has to be.

Mark

"Cody!"

A bunch of freshman freeze midstrip and stare, but I stomp right past them. Ordinarily I might stop and say hi to a couple of guys on the team, but not today. I've got a beef.

I find Cody and Mitch Castellano standing at the bank of lockers farthest from the door, the ones reserved for seniors. They are laughing and tossing out names—"Jenny Wright!" "Felicia!" "Fat Cassidy from choir!" It takes me a minute to realize what these girls have in common, and when I get it, I'm doubly pissed. The Cody I grew up with would never have lingered in locker rooms with his shirt off, admiring himself and laughing about girls too ugly for him to date.

I slam shut Cody's open locker. He jumps about a foot in the air. "Palmer! Jesus!"

"You fucking did it."

"Did what?"

"I *told* you not to Wild Card the new girl. And you fucking did it anyway."

Cody leans against his locker, propped up on one shoulder, which must be uncomfortable, but he makes it look natural, the smug bastard. "Mark, choosing the Wild Card is my job. I'm the class president. I get to pick. Me. Not you."

"She doesn't even know what Prom Bowl *is*!"

"I'm sure someone will tell her."

"Yeah, and they'll tell her she didn't even make the popular vote, that she's only in there because the class president is a fucking dickbasket."

"Oh, would you calm down?" Cody rolls his eyes so hard I'm surprised they don't escape his face. "There's always a Wild Card, dude. I didn't invent the concept. It was always going to be somebody. It's an important part of the contest. This way it's not just the predictable fifteen hot chicks. You get someone a little more . . . "

"More what?"

"Accessible."

"The fuck does *that* mean?"

"It means people can relate to her, nimrod. It means the guys who would never think of laying down money on Caity Pierce have a dog in the fight. It means the girls at this school who never had a chance of being picked have someone to root for."

"Yeah, because you care *so* much about unpopular girls."

"I care about *tradition*, and you should too. Anyway, I don't know what you're so twisted up about. It's good for her, too. She'll probably get a low bid in the first round, go out early, and have her prom date all lined up for her. She won't have to get all worked up about whether or not someone's going to ask her."

A damp towel flies over the bank of lockers and lands on the floor between us.

"What the hell?" I raise my voice. "Hey, who threw that?"

A kid edges his way around the corner, wary, biting his lip. "Sorry."

Cody raises his eyebrows. "You're on the JV team."

"I'm Chad."

"What the fuck are you throwing towels for, Chad?"

"I didn't. It was my buddy. I was—"

Cody grabs him by the shoulder and slams him against the lockers. "Don't fucking throw shit."

"Dude!" I grab Cody's arm and try to pull him off the kid, but Cody shoves as I pull and Chad ends up on the ground, huddled next to the towel and looking freaked as hell.

"Pick it up," Cody orders.

Chad does, scrambling to his feet.

"Towels go in the cart. Think you can remember that?"

"Y-yes."

"Don't let it happen again." Cody turns back to me. "Mark, you're the student council president. You're supposed to run this thing."

"I'm . . . hang on." I feel like I'm watching TV with my

grandmother, who has memory issues and gets bored with every program in about twelve seconds. Cody is changing channels too fast for me to keep up with the plot. I can't believe he shoved that kid down like that. Three years ago, Cody was the one getting pushed around by the seniors.

Tradition, I guess.

"You have to back my play here," Cody says, clearly not even thinking about Chad or the towel anymore. "And that means once I've picked a Wild Card, you don't go questioning it."

"Cody . . ."

The door to the locker room swings open. "Spencer? You in here?"

"Shit. That's Coach." Cody shoots me a panicked look and pulls his shirt over his head. I know what he's thinking, but Chad wouldn't have ratted him out, would he? You don't run and tell Coach. You take your lumps. It sucks, but that's the way it is. Hell, Cody always took his lumps. That's probably why he feels justified pushing little kids around now. I tag after him as he makes his way to the front of the locker room, where Coach is waiting in the doorway of his office.

Coach smiles when he sees me. "Palmer. Good game Friday."

"Thanks, Coach."

"Arm feeling good?"

"Yes sir."

"Have you been concentrating on your head alignment, like we talked about?"

"Yes sir."

"Good job, son. Head on out now. I need to talk to Spencer for a moment."

I go to my locker for my gym uniform, but I come back to the front of the locker room to change. I stand close to Coach's door like a creeper and eavesdrop. Because Cody's right, it is my responsibility to have his back, and if he's in trouble for what went down with that freshman . . . I mean, he didn't hurt the kid. Yeah, he pushed him around, it was a dick move, but Cody would never actually hurt anyone. Coach Vanguard is new. Maybe he doesn't know that this is the way things are, that the seniors sometimes beat on the freshmen a little, that it's obnoxious and mean but otherwise harmless. I'll tell him. If Cody's in trouble, I'll stick up for him.

Their voices are hard to hear, muffled by the door. ". . . back up Lewis," Coach says.

Lewis is our center, so that makes sense. Lewis handles the snap on most plays, but Cody subs in for the long snaps, for field goal attempts. But then Cody says, in a voice that carries, "You mean second string?"

Shit, what?

Coach's voice drops, and I press my ear against the door, straining to hear. "I'm sorry, son."

"Yeah. Whatever."

"You're still an important part of the team." But this is just a line and we both know it. Most of the second string players won't see a minute of playing time all year. God, I should have known when I saw Lewis working on his long snap that something was up. Cody's always been mediocre, but the guy tries. I can't believe Coach would demote him like this, take away his entire season and any chance he might have had at being noticed by a scout.

The door flies open and I jump out of the way just in time to avoid getting smacked in the face. Cody storms out.

I hurry after him. "Cody."

He doesn't answer.

"Cody, man, I heard—"

"We're late for class," he snaps, and shoves through the locker room door out into the gym, leaving me standing there staring after him.

3

Ava

“Can I sit down?”

I look up from my book. It’s Mark, the football player, easily recognizable by his mop of sandy hair and green eyes even though he’s not in uniform. He pulls out a chair and hovers over it, as if he knows I’m going to say yes and is just waiting for the formality.

I find my voice. “You aren’t in an independent study.”

He laughs. “I switched in. Starting today. Okay if I sit?”

“Oh. Right. Yeah.”

He swings easily into the chair. “What’s your project?”

“The space race.”

“That sounds made up.”

“It’s not made up!”

“It sounds like something from *Star Wars*.”

“It’s what they called it when NASA was originally trying to send men to the moon. We were in this competition with Russia, and this was during the Cold War, so everyone was kind of paranoid that whichever side won was going to put a bunch of nuclear weapons on the moon or something like that.”

He leans his chair back on two legs. "That *definitely* sounds made up."

"I mean, it was a little out there, yeah, but then we ended up making it to the moon using 1960s technology, which is hardcore. Like, the spacecraft that landed on the moon was lower-tech than your phone. Just think about that."

"You're pretty into this space stuff."

"I just like history a lot." My face heats up. "I guess that makes me a loser."

"No, it's cool. Being interested in stuff is cool. Not having interests is what makes someone a loser."

"You think?"

"Nothing more boring than an apathetic poser."

"What's your project?"

He shrugs. "Haven't picked yet. I'm here to get out of Calc."

"You don't like Calc?"

"I failed a couple of quizzes. Gotta keep my grades up so I don't become ineligible."

Of course. Half the library is filled with guys from the football team, doing independent studies on the history of the NFL or comparing Joe Montana's career with Peyton Manning's, dodging classes where they can't keep up.

"What's that face?" Mark's eyebrows furrow.

"What face?"

"You made a face."

I feel my cheeks burn. "I didn't mean to."

"You think I'm some dumb jock."

"No! I just . . . you know."

"What?"

"I don't think you're *dumb*. But my dad's been coaching since I was a little kid. I know how it works. Football players don't take hard classes because they can't risk failing. You can't risk an ineligibility. So you never learn Calc or AP Physics or anything like that. Sports are more important to you than an education."

Mark shakes his head. "Wow. You've got me all figured out, I guess."

"Well, you did think the Cold War was *made up*."

"I knew about the Cold War. I just thought you were making up the space chase."

"Space *race*."

"See, you can't tell me that name doesn't sound made up."

"I mean . . . *someone* made it up, at some point. It didn't emerge fully formed into the collective consciousness of the nation."

He laughs. Not like I'm a loser. Like he thinks I'm funny. Okay then.

"I didn't mean to insult you," I say. "I know you're not stupid."

"You do, huh?"

"I can tell from talking to you."

"I do care about school," he says. "I need to stay eligible to get scholarships so I can go to college."

I'm embarrassed. I never think about things like this, about the fact that college isn't a sure thing for everyone. That there are people—people like Mark, I guess—who have to consider everything they do in the context of how it will impact their future. I don't have to do that. I'm bright enough that a state school is a safe bet for me. I can probably aim higher if I want to, but I know Dad would love to see me in the Big Ten, would love to come to campus on game weekends and wear my colors and take me out to pub & grill dinners after victories. And I don't know a lot about our family's finances, exactly, but Sean and I get new clothes and new shoes and new computers when we ask for them. We have enough that I know for sure I'm going to college, even if I were to fail Calc.

"Sorry," I say to Mark.

"For what?"

"Acting like you're a meathead."

"It's okay. You just met me."

"Which is why I shouldn't act like I know what I'm talking about."

"The rest of the team, they're mostly like that," Mark admits. "They either think they're bound for the NFL—"

"Which, statistically speaking, *nobody* is."

"Right? Or else they're just so high on the fact that they're playing Varsity at Patterson that they can't see past the ends of their noses."

"Unlike you?"

"I love football. But no, I'm really about getting a college spot. I do volunteer work, I'm student council president . . . all that shit college admissions guys love. I mean, you're a senior. I'm sure you know the drill."

"You're student council president?" This is amazing. By sheer dumb luck I'm sitting next to one of the few people in the world who might be able to help me out of my situation, and if that weren't wild enough, we actually seem to be hitting it off.

"Don't get too excited. I don't have the power to cancel homework."

"Do you have the power to get me out of this Prom Bowl thingy?"

His smile disappears. "I thought you might not like that."

"So you knew."

"Well, everyone knows."

"How? It was announced on a private Facebook page."

"Yeah, the closet where Jen Folger hooked up with Brad Lennox was private too. Word gets around."

Brad Lennox, the placekicker Charlotte likes? I file that one away. "So can you get me out of it?"

He sighs. "Wish I could."

I feel like my throat is swelling shut. Damn it. I don't want to cry in the middle of this library full of strangers or in front of this boy. I want Mark to think I'm cool. He'll find me out eventually, for sure, but does it really have to be this soon?

"Hey," Mark says, "it's gonna be fine, you know? Prom Bowl's no big deal."

I swallow hard. "I don't see the point of it." Yeah, that's great. I sound like Nora Gates, this whiny tagalong girl who hung out with me and my friends back home. She'd plop down at our lunch table with tears in her eyes, going on about how she was *so over* some boy who she obviously wasn't over at all. You don't cry about something if you're over it. And this isn't about me seeing the point of Prom Bowl. I know that. Mark knows that. I wouldn't be biting my lip and trying not to cry about this if I was just a spectator.

He's watching me with soft eyes. "Do you want to take a walk?"

I do. I really, really do. "We aren't allowed to leave the library."

Mark raises a hand and flags the librarian. "Hey, Mr. H? I'm gonna show Ava where the nurse's office is. Cool?"

"Stay together," he says, like we're venturing off into the wilderness and one of us might get picked off by lions if we're not careful. It almost makes me laugh, but the laugh shakes a sob loose instead. I hate crying in public, particularly at school. I can never stop once I've started. It escalates, and eventually I'm just crying *because I'm crying*, and well-meaning teachers or classmates huddle around me and go, *What's wrong, Ava?* and I can't get my breathing and my voice under control to tell them this is just me, this is just a thing I do sometimes, and I am not as upset as I look, and if everyone would back off I'd get it together and be okay.

Mark leads the way out of the library, slightly ahead of me, which lets me pretend he hasn't noticed the tears I'm trying to wipe away.

"You don't really want to go to the nurse's office, do you?" he asks, once we're out in the hall.

"N-no."

"Cool tip—teachers will always let a girl out of any class if you say you need to see the nurse. They're afraid if they ask questions, you'll tell them you've got your period."

That actually does make me laugh a little. He's so earnest, like he's the first person to have discovered this phenomenon. "What about you? How come it was so easy for you to leave?"

"Oh, I'm the quarterback. I don't know if you knew that about me."

"Ha. Fair enough."

He falls back a little to walk alongside me. "Prom Bowl's been at Patterson longer than I have. It's a way of raising money for the prom, that's all."

"You're telling me this school can't afford to put on a prom? I think your stadium is actually better than Soldier Field."

"Where the Chicago Bears play? That place sucks."

"Okay, but they're a professional sports organization and Patterson's a public high school, so . . ."

He chuckles. "Yeah, point taken. I don't know, maybe the school couldn't afford its prom when the Prom Bowl was invented and now we just do it for the sake of tradition."

"This was supposed to be my anonymous year." I can't believe I'm telling him this. I haven't even told Dad and Sean this. "I just wanted one year where I wouldn't have to worry about what people were thinking about me, because they wouldn't be thinking about me at all."

"Yeah," he says. "I get that."

"*You* get that? You're, like, the most visible guy in the whole school."

"Well, yeah. Exactly. I'd love to turn that off for a while."

"Even though you'd lose your get-out-of-independent-study-free card?"

"Even though."

"So why don't you? Why don't you hang the jersey up?"

He shrugs. "Lots of reasons. I need the scholarship, like I told you. I love playing football. And . . . the team's counting on me." He cuts a glance at me. "You know what that's like? Having a team counting on you?"

"I don't play sports."

"Teams aren't just for sports."

"My dad," I say after a moment. "And Sean. That's my team."

"You'd do anything for them?"

"I moved here for them."

"You had a choice?"

"Dad said we'd all decide together. He said he'd understand if I didn't want to leave Carbondale right before senior year."

"You came anyway."

"I couldn't let him down."

He nods. "It's the same with the senior class. They've been

waiting for their prom for the past three years. Prom Bowl is a part of the experience. And everyone's counting on me to support it."

"But why can't you have it without me? I don't even understand how enough people know who I am to have voted for me for something like this."

"On the Facebook page, did you see the label by your photo?"

"Yeah, what does 'Wild Card' mean, anyway?"

"The Wild Card is like a draft pick." There's a hesitance in his voice.

"What are you saying? Someone chose me specifically? That's creepy."

"It's part of the tradition. The class president handpicks one contestant, to shake things up. To keep it interesting."

Something clunks into place, and I feel like I'm detaching from my body, from this girl who's standing in the hall talking to the quarterback like she has any right to do that. My voice sounds like it's coming from far away. "I didn't get the vote."

"No." He doesn't look at me.

That's why I don't look like the other girls. That's why the Prom Bowl is top-heavy with girls who aren't so . . . top-heavy. "I got picked to be the ugly one."

"No! Jeez, Ava, no." He rakes a hand through his hair. "It's because no one knows you, I think. You're mysterious. The rest of us, you know, we've mostly been together since kindergarten." His fingers find my arm, circle gently around my wrist, pull me to a stop, pull me back to myself. "There's something about a girl you didn't know when she was in pigtails. Something special."

He's wrong. If anything sets me apart from the masses, it's my ability to resist moves like this—except that I'm not resisting at all, I'm turning toward him. I'm letting him hold onto my arm even though we've stopped walking.

"That's a meathead thing to say," I find my voice. My words are mocking him, but my tone is something else altogether.

He smiles and lets my arm slip out of his grip.

Why is that disappointing?

Mark clears his throat and we start walking again. "You don't need me to get you out of Prom Bowl," he says. "It's challenges. Just throw the first challenge and you'll be out."

"What kind of challenges?" If it's something athletic, I won't need to throw it. I'll suck *au naturale*.

"Don't know. It's different every year. But all you have to do is not try hard at whatever it is, so nobody bids too much on you. The people who get the lowest bids are cut, and then you won't have to think about it anymore until prom night."

"Prom night? What happens then?"

"Well, you have to go to the prom with whoever bought you."

"So getting out in the first round won't get me out of that."

"No, but it'll get you out of having to compete anymore. Plus, the early cuts usually get bought up by the kind of guys who don't mind a low-profile date. They'll take you to the Olive Garden and have you home before midnight. The high rollers will all be holding out for the top five girls."

"I could get stuck with a jerk."

"Or you could get a really nice guy."

"This is gross."

"I'll even help." He takes my hand again, gives it a little squeeze. It's reassuring. It strikes me, suddenly, that *Mark* is probably a really nice guy.

Okay, I'm getting carried away.

"This isn't going to be a big deal," Mark says. "I promise you."

"Pretty confident."

"Yeah, well."

"You're the quarterback. Yeah, I've heard."

We turn a corner and are back outside the library. I was completely wrong about where we were in the building. When is this place going to stop being so confusing?

"We should go back in," I say, pausing in front of the door. But I'm still not pulling free of Mark's hand. Exactly what am I doing? I can't walk into a room full of football players holding hands with their quarterback. That's the least invisible thing a girl could possibly do.

"Ava?"

"Yeah?"

"Do you want to come see a movie with me this weekend?"

"Um. What movie?"

Oh, nice, Ava. Because *that's* the salient factor. Sure, cute boy, I'll go out with you, but *only if I like the movie*. Otherwise you're on your own!

Mark laughs. I want to dissolve into my constituent atoms. "Whatever you want."

"Okay. Yes."

"Give me your phone."

I do. He types for a minute and hands it back. "Call me." And with a jaunty wave, dips back into the library before I have time to respond.

I have to call *him*?

Why do bad things happen to good people?

4

Ava

It took me almost two hours to find Mark's entry in my cell phone, because he didn't enter himself under M for "Mark" or P for "Palmer," but rather Q for "Quarterback." It took me another day and a half to decide whether that was obnoxious or cute.

I think I'm going with cute.

Now I just have to get up the nerve to call him.

I know the stigma about a girl who spends her Saturday nights doing puzzles in her room. I know it from Dad, actually—sometime around the middle of my sophomore year, he picked up a habit of poking his head into my room and watching me for a few minutes with this disturbed look on his face. Last year, after Mom left, he started asking me along to the football games and encouraging me to sit in the bleachers instead of behind the bench with him and Sean. Flyers for Carbondale's under-eighteen dance club also started randomly appearing in my room.

Okay, Dad, I get it. You've got an uncool daughter.

But the truth is that I *like* having Saturday nights to myself. I like hanging out in my room with reruns of *Friends* and orange sodas, and staying up until two or three in the morning in my own little oasis. I don't love being seen as a boring loser, but if the alternative is wasting my weekend at a dark, sticky-floored club with no chill . . . well, it's no contest. The heart wants what it wants, and my heart wants jammies and me time.

However.

My heart also, apparently, is not going to let go of the memory of Mark's fingers on my wrist or his hand in mine.

How can fingers on my arm be so exciting? I circle my own fingers around my wrist. Nothing. No spark. Of course not.

Could he really like me?

God, wouldn't that be weird.

It's not that I think I'm repugnant or anything. But you hear about those girls who never date, and then they come into their own in college, and I always figured I'd be one of those girls. Not the kind who gets asked out by a quarterback her second week at a new school.

I can't call him. It's too intimidating. I text instead. Movie tonight? That's casual, right? Ugh, maybe I should have used two question marks so I wouldn't look like such a punctuation freak. But then that would look desperate, like begging. Oh God.

I can't sit here staring at my phone waiting for an answer or I'll go crazy, so I shut it in my desk drawer and go downstairs. Dad's watching footage of the Carbondale High season opener from last year. I plop down on the couch beside him and wait to be acknowledged.

Dad pauses, rewinds a few seconds, and hits play. The Carbondale wide receiver misses a pass.

"The throw was bad," Dad says, as if we were already talking about this, as if I'd asked. "Carbondale had a weak team. Now, Palmer's got a real gift. Might actually see a winning season this year, with him at the helm."

"Yeah?"

"Kid can put a ball exactly where he wants it."

"Dad, can we talk?"

"Sure."

"Can you pause this?"

For a minute I think he's not going to. He lets the play end and the next one start. I'm about to leave and come back later, maybe go check my phone, when he mutes the TV but leaves the video running. "What's up, kid?"

"Dad, when you went to Patterson—"

"Oh, come on, ham-hands! That throw was perfect!"

"Dad."

"Sorry." He finally turns off the TV. "When I went to Patterson?"

"Well, did . . . was there a thing called the Prom Bowl?"

His face lights up. "God, the Prom Bowl! I forgot all about that!"

"So they did have it?"

"Sure they had it. It was a school tradition. You mean it's still going on?"

"Well, I'm kind of . . . in it."

He frowns. "In it how? What do you mean?"

"I mean, I'm a contestant."

"Oh." Dad rubs his chin, stroking a beard he doesn't have. "Huh. How do we feel about that?"

"It's weird, don't you think? I mean, boys are going to be bidding on me as a date."

"Is this still a fundraiser? In my day all the money went toward paying for the prom."

"Yeah, I think that's right. That's what I was told." I don't mention my doubts about whether Patterson needs help paying for their prom or not. I know what Dad would say about the relative importance of a senior prom versus a high-class football stadium.

"Well, if that's the case." Dad reaches for the remote. "Sounds like it's all in good fun."

"You think so?"

"Sure. You'll stay out of trouble, won't you?"

"When have I ever gotten in trouble?"

"That's my good girl." He perks up. "Hey, you'll get a date out of it, kid."

I have to bite back the retort that's on the tip of my tongue—*I already got a date!* I don't have a date, not really, and I wouldn't be able to stand the humiliation if Mark blew me off and my dad knew about it. Instead I say, "It seems like a pretty crazy tradition. You don't think so?"

"Most traditions are," he says sagely. "Have you ever really stopped to think about Easter eggs?"

"I guess."

"Look, talk to Charlotte. Or one of your other friends. I'm sure they'll be able to put your mind at ease about this."

"Well yeah, I actually talked to Mark a little."

Dad puts the remote back down. Suddenly, I have his full attention. "Mark Palmer?"

"Uh-huh."

"How do you know Mark Palmer?"

Sometimes it's like he's completely blind to the fact that his players and my classmates are the same people. "He's in my fifth period independent study."

"Dropped that calculus class, huh?"

"Yeah."

"And what did he have to say?"

"That a lot of people get out in the first round. That if I don't want to be part of the Prom Bowl, I can just not try very hard."

"Ava. Are you talking about throwing the competition?"

Crap. I should have known better than to mention that. Not giving a hundred and ten percent is a capital offense in Dad's world. "Mark said it would be okay," I mumble. "He said he would help me."

"Oh Ava, don't pull Mark into this."

I can't stand it when Dad sounds so disappointed. I knit my fingers together and wait for judgment.

"I know you've had a tough time. We all have since Mom left. Yeah?"

I don't want to talk about this. We never talk about this. I want to go up to my room and stare at my phone until it rings. I want to not be having this conversation. "Yeah."

"And I know it was hard on you, moving away from your friends and your school right before senior year."

"It's okay, Dad."

"You're a key member of this team, you know."

"Yeah, I know."

"So I want you to be honest with me. Is Mark Palmer in charge of the Prom Bowl?"

Are we talking about Mark? I thought we were talking about my mom. I don't really want to talk about Mark either, but I have to admit it's the lesser of two evils, and anyway I did bring him up. "I don't think he's . . . in *charge*, per se. He's the student council president, so he's probably got his hands in everything."

"Ava, you know, if something happens and Mark isn't able to fulfill all his responsibilities, the first thing the school will do is pull him from the football team."

"What are you saying, Dad?"

"The team needs Mark to win games. I need him to have a successful season, so I can nail this job for you and Seanie."

I don't get it. "What do you want me to do about it?"

"If it's Mark's responsibility to make sure the Prom Bowl runs smoothly, don't make waves. For me. Okay, kiddo?" He squeezes my shoulder. "Just go along with it. I bet you'll even have some fun."

I don't know what to say. I will not have some fun. I hate that my father thinks I'm so pathetic, that he's so set on the idea that I'm this sad girl and I'd be fixed if I integrated myself into more football-esque activities. Doesn't he think I'm smart enough to know my own mind? And shouldn't he be on my side? Shouldn't he be more concerned with me than with Mark's extracurricular responsibilities?

But I don't know. Maybe it makes sense. It's not like Dad's ever asked me for anything—not until recently, that is. Since my mom left, what have my contributions *really* been? Doing the laundry occasionally? Helping Sean with his algebra? And it's nice that Dad's telling me this stuff. It's like he finally sees me as an adult, as someone who can be relied on to help carry the weight of the family. I have to admit that part of me was a little disappointed when it turned out Dad didn't need me to take over the cooking. I wanted to help. Maybe this is my chance to do that.

"Okay Dad. I'll try."

"That's my girl." He turns back to the TV and I recognize my cue to leave.

I get back to my room just in time to see the light on my phone screen fade to black. I snatch it up and stab at the bottom button. There, like finding a two-dollar bill, is the elusive text from Quarterback Mark Palmer: Like horror movies?

I would have said yes to anything. I would have said yes if

he'd asked me to go tour the water treatment plant. But, as it happens, I love horror movies.

Sure, I text back, because it's not like I'm going to talk about love with Mark Palmer before we've even been on a date.

Pick you up at 7

I flop down on my bed, feeling like I've run a marathon. I have a date, a real date, with Mark Palmer. Now I just have to do whatever I can to discourage people from bidding on me in whatever the first challenge turns out to be.

For a minute, I imagine Mark bidding on me, some token amount that doesn't even matter so it won't feel sketchy. This could actually turn out okay. I just have to blow off the contest.

What Dad doesn't know won't hurt him.

Mark

"So hang on, break this down for me," I say. "The chef from the diner and the clown at the kid's birthday were the same guy?"

Ava laughs. She's cute when she laughs. She's cute when she doesn't laugh, too, don't get me wrong, but I especially like her laugh. "You didn't know they were the same guy? Not even when he went psycho on everyone at the party with the steak knife?"

"You're saying I should have known he was the chef because he had a steak knife? Anybody could have a steak knife. My grandma has steak knives. That's not conclusive."

She gives me epic side-eye. "Are you messing with me? You really didn't know?"

I don't answer. I try not to let my face show anything, but my lips want to smile, and I end up pulling them into a weird lemon-sucking contortion.

"You're *messing* with me!" She belts me in the arm. She sounds fucking delighted, like me trolling her is the highest compliment she could have received. Which is sort of sad, but also sort of flattering. I don't know.

"You want to go in here?" We're passing Sonny's Side Up, which is this nutty baseball-themed place run by a guy who's older than God. Sonny's cool, though. I think he must be a huge sports fan, because he always gives members of the football team free drinks.

"You want to go to a diner?" Ava raises her eyebrows. "Seriously?"

"It's okay. I know the guy who runs it. I promise he's not a mass murdering clown."

"But, like, you didn't know the guy in the movie was the mass murdering clown either, so how can I trust you?" She smirks.

"C'mon." I push the door open. "I really need some nachos."

Sonny's is laid out kind of like a train car—one long aisle with booths on either side. The walls are covered with cool memorabilia, like an autographed Reggie Jackson card, and also a lot of pointless crap like mitts and home plates. The floors are sticky with spilled pop that Sonny never quite cleans up all the way. I watch Ava take this in.

"Do we just sit anywhere?" she asks.

"C'mon." I pull her to the back left corner, which is the farthest you can get from the door. "I always sit here."

"You come here a lot?"

As if in answer, Sonny himself appears at our table. "Mark!"

"Hey Sonny."

"Coke or Dr Pepper?"

"Coke, please."

"On the house! And what will your lady friend have?"

"Uh, what will you have?" I redirect the question to Ava, since Sonny's eyes are still on me.

"Coke Zero?" Ava asks.

Sonny's still waiting. "Coke Zero," I tell him.

"One Coke and one Coke Zero!" He slaps a couple of menus down heartily and disappears into the kitchen.

Ava raises her eyebrows. "Wow."

"What?"

"You sure do get a lot of perks."

"You're the coach's daughter. You're telling me you don't get any perks?"

She pulls the ramekin of sugar packets toward her and starts organizing. "I get free Gatorade on game nights. Is that a perk?"

"If you like Gatorade."

"I hate Gatorade."

"How can you hate Gatorade?"

"Oh, you'd hate it too if you'd had all the Gatorade you could drink since you were four years old."

"Really? Since you were four?"

"Yeah, that's when Dad got his first coaching job. He was just an assistant back then, but then the Carbondale head coach retired and Dad took over."

"So you're really, like, a football brat."

"Is that like an Army brat?"

"Yeah, I just made it up. Do you like it?"

"Pretty fitting. I do get sick of moving."

"After that long, I imagine you'd be pretty sick of the whole football scene." Actually, I can't imagine that at all. I never seem to get sick of football. When we were kids, Cody and I used to hide in trees when our parents came looking for us, so we'd be able to stay out later and play a little longer. But Ava doesn't strike me as a big football fan. It's hard to imagine her in a cheerleader uniform, or even in the bleachers. She definitely looked more at home in the library the other day.

"Yeah," she says. "But, you know. Football's part of the family."

"That's a funny way to put it."

"It's just the truth. That's how it's always been. Football's like the third parent. Or, well, the second parent, I guess."

She looks a little uncomfortable, and I think maybe I should let it go, but she wouldn't have mentioned it if she didn't want to talk about it, right? "Your mom?"

"Ditched us a year ago."

"Oh, I'm sorry."

She shrugs. "We're getting used to it."

"How come you live with your dad?"

"Because he can't manage without me."

"Ha. Naturally."

"She left the family," Ava says, the smile fading from her face. "That doesn't mean the family stops existing. It just means she doesn't want to be in it."

"So where is she now? Not around here?"

"No, she's married to some guy in Carbondale."

"Where you used to live?"

"Yeah."

"Is he nice, at least?"

"Who knows? I've never met him."

"Not even at the wedding?"

"Didn't go." She pushes the sugar ramekin away and starts on the creamers. "I haven't seen her since she left."

"Not at all? She didn't even try for custody or anything?"

"Wouldn't have mattered if she did. I don't want to see her."

"Really?"

"I feel like it would be, I don't know, cheating on my dad. Sean sees her sometimes—you know, my little brother, Sean?—but I don't."

"Man. Sucks." I get pissed off at my mom all the time, but I can't imagine cutting her off like that. On the other hand, I can't imagine her walking out on our family. I guess I should consider myself lucky.

"She left us first," Ava says. "Made leaving her pretty easy."

Sonny comes back with our Cokes and a dish of lemons. "All set here?"

"Give us a few minutes," I tell him. Ava hasn't even looked at the menu.

"You don't want nachos?" Sonny asks. I always get nachos. Sonny's no fool.

"Probably. We haven't decided."

He claps me on the shoulder. "I'll get you some nachos."

"Okay, Sonny."

"Nachos for me too," Ava decides.

Sonny laughs. "I like her. Good girl!"

"Um. Thank you?" Ava raises her eyebrows at me.

I shrug, even though I know what Sonny's doing. I've never brought a date here. The girls who usually come to Sonny's with me are cheerleaders and occasionally Cody's hookups, all of whom gravitate toward things like ice water and salads. Sonny appreciates a girl with a healthy appetite. A healthy wallet, too.

"I'm sorry," I say, once he's out of earshot. "About your mom, I mean."

"Thanks."

Most people would have said *it's okay,* or maybe *don't worry about it*. I like that Ava didn't. "I didn't mean to pry."

"You didn't. It was a year ago. I'm mostly used to it."

"Your dad's lucky to have you on his side."

She motions toward the dish of lemons, asking, and I push them toward her because who wants lemons in their Coke? Gross.

"I just want him to be happy," she says. "It's been so long since he's really been happy. Maybe it's dumb, but I feel like if there's anything I can do for him, I should do it."

"Yeah, I get that. My parents want me to go to Notre Dame."

"Good football school."

"Yeah, so they keep telling me."

"Good school generally."

"Yup."

She reads my tone. "You don't want to go?"

"Nah, I don't know. They're not scouting me. And I've got some other offers. I'd like to just say yes to someplace, you know?"

"But you don't want to let your parents down?"

"I don't want to pass up a chance to make them happy."

"I'm sure they will be," Ava says. "How could they not? You're the star of the team. You're going to get a scholarship to somewhere, even if it doesn't turn out to be Notre Dame. My dad says you're the best quarterback he's ever seen at the high school level."

Really? "Coach Vanguard said that?"

"Well, he didn't exactly say it." She blushes a little, adorably. "I just know what he's thinking."

Sonny arrives with two plates of nachos, hot and covered in cheese, beef, and jalapeños. I lift a chip and extend it toward her. "Cheers."

She taps a chip of her own against mine and devours it in a single bite, getting nacho cheese all over her chin in the process.

• • •

So what's my next move here?

I'm supposed to be writing a letter of interest to the athletic program at Notre Dame, but Ava won't get out of my head. Coach is going to kill me, and that's only if my parents don't beat him to it. I'm not supposed to be thinking about girls. It's senior year. I'm supposed to be acing my classes, winning games, netting scholarships. It's all been for nothing if I lay an egg in the end zone, as Dad would say.

But God, she's cute.

She's cute, and fun, and hilarious, and this is my senior year. I deserve a little fun, right? I haven't had a serious relationship all through high school. And I always figured I'd go to prom with a bunch of guys, or maybe bite the bullet and ask Amy Spicoli, but I can't stop picturing Ava on my lap in the back of a limo, Ava letting me hold her for a slow dance to some nineties cheese, Ava in the pool at Caity Pierce's after-prom party. I bet she's hot in a bikini. She'd be good in a chicken fight too, tough to knock off my shoulders. We'd beat Cody and whatever girl he's with, and then we'd wrap up in a big towel and go lie in a pool chair to watch the sun come up, and maybe fall asleep for awhile. Or maybe we'd go inside and up to one of the rooms in Caity's parents' giant house, and I'd pull a tie on her bikini top and it would slip off her and—

Fuuuck.

Coach is definitely, definitely going to kill me.

And, shit, none of this matters anyway, because the bigger

problem that *I swear* only just occurred to me is that Ava is in the Prom Bowl and whoever takes her to prom is going to have to lay down some serious cash. Even the first-round girls usually go for around a hundred dollars. Where am I going to get that? Mowing lawns? Not in effing October.

So what can I do? Ask her out and let some other guy take my girlfriend to the prom? Let some other guy play with her in the pool at Caity Pierce's after-prom party?

I should just get her out of the Prom Bowl. It's what she wants.

But I can't do that. I can't interfere in the Bowl. I promised Cody. I can't undermine him. Especially not now, after what happened with Coach.

I wonder if he'd loan me some money?

That's an idea, actually. Cody's mom is some kind of big shot attorney, so they've got boatloads of money. Like, they have a literal boat. It mostly sits in their giant four-car garage, but Cody's dad has let a bunch of us take it up to Lake Superior on fishing trips a couple of times. We spend the day on the lake and come home with sunburns and hangovers and several pounds of freshwater salmon, most of which ends up at my house because if my mom has a freezer full of fresh fish she'll actually look up recipes, whereas Cody's family will get bored of salmon and throw it away.

But I don't really want to ask Cody for money. It's never been weird that his family has money and mine doesn't, and it seems like the kind of thing that could so easily come between us.

Cody's always been great at spreading the wealth without crossing the line into charity. He got me onto his family's phone plan when my parents couldn't afford to buy us smartphones, but he's not always picking up the tab at restaurants or anything like that. Anyway, if I asked him to help me pay for Ava, I know I'd spend all of prom feeling like he was the one who really bought her.

Which puts me back at square one.

God, everything really is set up to favor people with money. It's not just colleges, which are totally going to accept Cody, bad grades and all, because his parents can shell out the tuition. I'm not even going to be able to take the girl I like to prom.

No, this can't be hopeless. Come on, I'm Mark Fucking Palmer, student council president and Quarterback Extraordinaire. I run 5Ks and make student films and volunteer on the weekends. I won the Milk Challenge sophomore year and didn't even get detention or throw up in the cafeteria trash can. I can come up with a hundred bucks to take a girl to prom.

Ava better not last beyond the first round, though, or I'm screwed.

PATTERSON HIGH PROM BOWL

Private

Cody Spencer

Posted 1 week ago

PROM BOWL FASHION SHOW
Homecoming night, 6 pm sharp
Patterson High Gym

When bidding on a lady, a gentleman wants to know how she presents herself. Are you going to show up to prom in a nasty dress with bad hair? If you can't dress to impress, you may not live to see round two!

Like • Reply

Amy Spicoli, Charlotte Ramsey, and 4 others like this

Mark Palmer

Good luck tonight!

Posted 30 min ago • **Like • Reply**

Cody Spencer, Caity Pierce, and 13 others like this

MEMBERS

Cody Spencer
Mark Palmer
Caity Pierce
Amy Spicoli
Marlee Wheeler
Solstice Downing
Emily Hickman

Denise Mellibosky
Maria Baker
Sarah Leavett
Charlotte Ramsey
Olivia Merchant
Hannah Bauman
Kylie Richards
Elizabeth Kepler
Joanna York
Wild Card: Ava Vanguard

5

Ava

"Want me to straighten your hair?" Charlotte waves the flatiron uncomfortably close to my face.

I jump back a little. "What for?" She's already spent ten minutes curling my eyelashes, and as far as I can tell they look exactly the same. "I thought you liked my hair."

She exhales hard, like I am the stupidest person alive. "I *do*, Ava, but I've also seen it about a hundred times. And so has everyone else. You need to make a *splash* tonight."

"A splash."

"Yes, a splash. You need to make everyone sit up and take notice."

"I don't think I'm a very splashy person, Charlotte."

"Ava." She snaps her fingers in my face. "Focus."

"You sound like my dad."

"You are *Ava Vanguard*. You were chosen for the Prom Bowl your second week at Patterson, when no one even knew who you were. You are the splashiest splasher who ever splashed."

"Seriously. You should give pep talks to athletes. Patterson probably wouldn't have lost yesterday with that kind of motivational spirit."

"How's your dad dealing?" she asks.

"The first loss of the season is always hard." It's not usually this hard, though. Dad went straight up to his room last night and didn't come out until two p.m. today, and that was just to grab a beer. I heard him through the door, on the phone with the assistant coaches, going over plays, trying to figure out what happened. I hope he doesn't think it's because I interfered with Mark's focus. "He really wanted an undefeated season," I tell Charlotte.

"Dream big."

"Yeah, well, that's Dad."

"So?" She waves the hair straightener again, like she's offering a steak to a cartoon dog.

"Yeah, okay."

"Do you know how to do it?"

"You said you were going to do it."

"Well, not if you know *how*. I have to get dressed too, you know. I can't spend all evening on you."

"I did not force you to do my makeup," I point out.

"You kind of did. Showing up all . . ." she waves her palm around my face in a wax-on-wax-off motion, meant to imply God only knows what.

I take the iron from her. "I can handle it."

"Cool." She strips off her shirt and sashays into her en-suite bathroom, leaving the door cracked open. Is she showing off, or is she just unaware of her own flawlessness? Does she know I'm staring at her? Does she ever think about the fact that her bra straps and panty lines are snug against her skin without being tight and causing ugly fat rolls and bulges? Does she even know fat rolls and bulges are a thing?

"Have you been to a homecoming dance before?" she asks. Her voice is all echoey with bathroom acoustics, making her sound farther away than she is.

"Of course."

"Sorry. You just don't seem like the school dance type."

How can I be offended? She's right. I'm not the school dance type. I went to homecoming one time, freshman year, when I was still figuring out who my friends were and how the high school scene worked. I hugged the wall for two hours and watched girls who looked like Charlotte dance with boys who looked like Mark. Then I went outside and called my mom to come pick me up.

Which won't be an option tonight.

Charlotte glides out of the bathroom like she's on ice. "Zip me up?"

I move behind her. The dress is like something off a runway—rose-colored satin hugs her torso from her breasts to her hips, where it abruptly fans out over layers and layers of tulle. The hemline is finely embroidered with an intricate vinelike pattern that crawls up onto the body of the skirt, making it look like Charlotte has just finished twirling. "How did you afford this?"

"Promise you won't tell?"

Her grin makes me nervous. "Tell who? Tell them what?"

Charlotte eases her bedroom door closed and turns to me. "I snaked my mom's credit card."

"You stole from your mom?"

"Borrowed, Ava. Jesus, keep your voice down."

I don't want to know this. "Are you going to pay her back?"

"Right. Where am I going to get nine hundred dollars?"

"Nine *hundred* dollars?"

"Will you calm down?"

"Charlotte, you know people get credit card statements in the mail, right? Your mom might even check her statement online before then. When she sees this charge—"

"Okay, seriously, you need to relax." She puts her hands on my shoulders. "I'm returning the dress tomorrow, okay? Mom is out with Dad at some play tonight. The charge will be gone before she has a chance to notice it."

"I don't know . . ."

"Ava, I do this all the time. It's fine."

Reluctantly, I nod.

She waves her hands at my garment bag. "Show me yours."

"It's not really in league with yours."

"Where'd you get it?"

"The Chrome Cricket."

I watch her consciously keep her nose from wrinkling. The Chrome Cricket is this funky, arty place a block from school that sells handcrafted pottery and kitschy sunglasses and things like that. I could see Charlotte going in for a laugh, but not for a homecoming dress.

Of course, my circumstances are unique.

I pull the bag off the bed and work open the knot at the bottom. The dress is a cotton one-size-fits-all number, elastic at the top and loose below the bustline. I believe there are people who would look very good in this dress, but I am not one of them.

Charlotte frowns. "Is that tie-dye?"

"It's from the craftsman class at the community college." I got that little fact from a printed card that was handed to me when I bought the dress. "Pretty neat, right?"

"The brown will bring out your eyes." Charlotte is really trying hard. Eighty percent of this dress is a murky green color. The brown is just accent. It was the ugliest dress I could find.

I hold it up to myself. The unstretched elastic doesn't even cover the front of my body. "What do you think?"

"Ava . . . ," Charlotte shakes her head. "Maybe my mom has something you can wear."

"No, I'm wearing this." I clutch my ugly dress like I love it.

"Ava, it's a *fashion show*. This is not fashion. This barely counts as clothes."

"It's okay, Charlotte."

"You're not going to last two seconds in that thing."

I close my eyes. "Maybe I don't want to last two seconds."

She's quiet for a little too long. "What?"

"Charlotte, listen—"

"What are you talking about?"

"I don't want to be in the Prom Bowl, all right?"

"I told you, everyone voted already. It's all decided. The first event is *tonight*."

She's not getting it. Maybe she can't get it; I don't know. This competition means enough to her that she'd steal her mother's credit card and charge a nine-hundred-dollar dress, so how can I expect her to understand that I want no part of it? God, Charlotte's probably been thinking about this since she was a freshman. And since Patterson apparently doesn't bother with naming a homecoming queen, the Prom Bowl is her only chance to win a crown.

She should really thank me. By taking myself out of the running, I'm making her odds of winning that much better. I'm not up for fighting with her, though. I take my dress and head into the bathroom to change. In a few hours, this will all be over anyway.

I hope.

Being at school after hours is always exciting. Even though it's Patterson and I'm new, walking down the darkened, empty hallway gives me the familiar sensation that the place belongs to me alone. The two thousand other people who share it with me during the day are irrelevant. That janitorial floor wax smell, the way the lockers feel as I run my fingers along their faces, the row of UN flags painted onto the bricks opposite the gym—they're all mine. I do a little running leap, just because I can, just because there is no one here to stop me.

Ms. Loren, the choir director, pokes her head out of a practice room. "Charlotte, Ava."

I freeze.

Ms. Loren smiles. "Don't you girls look lovely."

Apparently I am not in trouble then. Also, Ms. Loren needs her vision (or perhaps her integrity) checked. I do not look lovely. The tie-dye dress is performing exactly as I'd hoped. I look like ten pounds of ham in a five-pound sack.

"The other girls are getting ready in one-oh-one." She points. The lights of room 101 are on, and I can hear the low hum of excited chatter. "Why don't you two join them? Someone will be along to fetch you when it's time."

"Everyone else is here already?" I ask. Charlotte mentioned without shame on the drive over that she was hoping to be here last, to make an entrance in her dress. But having all eyes on me sounds like a nightmare.

"Every one of you," Ms. Loren smiles a faraway smile. "You girls all look so lovely in these gowns."

All but one of us. I can't help thinking it. I know it was deliberate. I chose this horrible dress on purpose, and I had a good reason. But nobody else is going to know that. And everyone in this whole school is going to see me in it.

I follow Charlotte down the hall, no longer feeling like I own the place. This school belongs to those distant girls in that lighted room who don't even know I exist, who are getting ready to parade themselves before a student body that collectively chose them as the most beautiful, the most desirable, the most deserving. They aren't Wild Cards, randomly picked by some boy to keep things interesting. They aren't the scrappy little no-account underdog.

Then we enter the classroom, and I get my first look at them.

Waves of soft hair. Long legs. Smooth skin. I feel like I'm in a museum of female perfection, and my first instinct is to stand there and take in the exhibits. They are skinnier than me. All but three are blonde. All but one are white. Charlotte joins the crowd, and I can see immediately that while she's holding her own, she is not the most beautiful girl here. She's short like me, and nobody else in this room is under five-foot-six. It makes the two of us look like children playing dress-up.

Well, one of us looks like she's playing dress-up. I look more like I'm wearing a smock for painting.

A girl in a wine-red bubble dress notices me standing by the wall. "Are you looking for the gym? I think everyone's supposed to go to the gym."

"Um, no, I'm Ava Vanguard. I'm um, competing. In the Prom Bowl?" I do not belong here. I *do not do not do not* belong here. I didn't need to wear this horrible dress to ensure my elimination tonight. All I needed to do was show up, with my big nose and my big hair and my big ass.

The girl looks me up and down and I can tell she's thinking along the same lines. She shrugs and turns her back to me to rummage through a pink makeup caboodle. Over her shoulder, I see dozens of partially used products. My own makeup bag at home contains two lipsticks, one neutral-toned eyeshadow palette, and a mascara wand. As if I needed more confirmation that I'm a different breed.

I want Charlotte. I want someone to protect me. But Charlotte is in the far corner of the room with an incredibly toned black girl who looks like the sun probably shines out of her pores. I sidle closer to them, hoping to be included, or at least introduced.

"Can you believe Laura didn't make the cut?" Charlotte is saying.

"You didn't hear?"

"Hear what?"

The girl lowers her voice. *"Chlamydia."*

"No! Kylie! Who told you that?"

"Amy. But everyone knows."

"Oh my God, was she cheating on Ian?"

"Must have been."

"Oh my *God*."

"I mean, who's going to bid on her now? Of course she wasn't picked."

"That's so disgusting!" Charlotte squeals. She sounds delighted. I have no idea how to join this conversation. I back away.

What am I supposed to be doing, exactly? The other girls are working on their hair and makeup, but I just spent hours on that stuff at home. I watch Charlotte take a seat and turn her face upward for the girl she's with, who is brandishing an eye pencil.

Do these girls ever stop putting the finishing touches on themselves?

"Ten minutes, ladies!" Ms. Loren is standing in the doorway behind me. "Amy, unplug your curling iron. Denise, would you like me to lock up your computer until after the dance?"

A curly-haired girl in a black scrap of dress hands Ms. Loren her laptop. When she bends over to pick it up, I glimpse her underwear. It's as barely-there as the dress, thin and lacy and smooth on her tanned, unlumpy skin.

My God, I am staring up this girl's skirt.

I am freaking out.

"I need some air." I push past Ms. Loren, out into the hallway. I need to get outside. I need to get away from these girls who seize on one another's flaws. I need to get away from the gym full of my classmates, waiting to watch me parade around in the world's ugliest dress. And part of me is sure that once I feel the night air on my face, I'll keep on going, all the way back to my brightly lit bedroom and my down comforter, my pajamas and my puzzles. They can't make me do this. Nobody can force me. What are they going to do?

Something cold and wet slaps me in the face and the chest.

What the hell?

I stop in my tracks, gasping, blinking, trying to comprehend.

Snowball?

In October, you moron?

I hear the receding beat of footsteps and open my eyes. A boy

I don't know is running away from me, clutching a big convenience store cup. As I watch, he rounds a corner and the sound of his footsteps fades out.

A trickle runs down my face and I catch it on my tongue. Cherry.

I've been slushy'd.

I look down at my horrible dress. The top is stained bright red, a humiliating target right across my breasts.

I lean against the lockers for a minute. I feel like maybe I'm going to pass out. This is straight out of a nightmare.

Why would someone do this?

Because you're a joke.

Because you're a Wild Card.

They don't want you in their Prom Bowl. Nobody voted for you. Nobody chose you. You're just here to keep it interesting. *Well, this is interesting. Court-jester interesting.*

I have to get out of here, right now.

"Ava? Honey? What are you—"

I turn toward the voice without thinking.

Ms. Loren gasps. "Ava, my God, what happened?"

Even as I make the decision that I am not going to cry, I can feel the tears coming. Ms. Loren crosses the space between us in two steps and crushes me against her and I stiffen. I hate teacher hugs. I hate being hugged when I'm trying not to cry. I hate this stupid day, this stupid school, this stupid town.

"Let's get you out of that dress," Ms. Loren whispers.

"I don't h-h-have anything else." God, I sound like I'm having some kind of breakdown. It's fine. I'm going to be *fine*. I just need to go home.

"We'll find you something."

I want to argue. I want to pull away from her and escape. But I don't trust my voice. If I try to speak, I'll cry again. Before I can pull myself together, Ms. Loren has me by the hand and we're marching through a greenroom that smells like sawdust and stage makeup, and then we're in a tiny room full of clothes hanging from rods that extend across every wall.

Ms. Loren flips through a rack and makes a selection. "Here you go, honey. Put this on."

I step back and shake my head.

"What's wrong?"

"I-I . . ." Damn it. I breathe in and out slowly, trying to calm myself. "I think I'm j-just gonna go home."

"Oh Ava. Don't let one cruel person ruin this experience for you," she says.

Is she going to hug me again? I wrap my arms around my torso, preventively. "I just don't think I want to. . . ."

"Think of all those girls out there, wishing they were you." Her eyes close briefly. "Girls dream of being in the Prom Bowl, Ava. You don't want to let those girls down. You owe it to them to make the most of this night."

"I . . ."

She presses the dress into my arms. "Hurry and get changed

now. It's almost time." And she's gone, leaving me alone with this dress and, apparently, the hopes and dreams of all the girls in school.

I don't owe them anything. She may be brainwashed, but I'm not. I don't have to do this just because other girls dream of it. I could hang this dress back up, go upstairs and out the door in the social sciences department, and walk home.

I totally could.

But the idea of walking home in the cold Minnesota night air in my slushy-soaked dress and facing Dad's disappointment is somehow marginally more horrible than this fashion show. The only thing he's asked me to do this year is to not make waves, and walking out on Patterson's cherished Prom Bowl tradition is probably more on the level of a monsoon. I can do this for Dad. He's been through so much, with the divorce. He needs to rely on me. And, I don't know, I can always wear this loaner dress home if I need to and return it on Monday.

I'll just try it on. That's not a commitment. It probably won't even fit, and if it doesn't, well, that'll be that.

6

Mark

"Mark!"

At first I can't find the source of the voice in all the chatter around me, but then I do. Murph Williams is picking his way through the bleachers and waving his arms over his head, so he's really kind of hard to miss once you get your head pointed in the right direction. I wave him over.

Murph is the most promising freshman quarterback in our county. Rumor has it that his parents scouted football programs and moved to the north side of town so Murph could play for Patterson. I wonder every time I see the kid how much of that is true, and how much I, as the current QB, factored into the decision. All I can say for sure is that Murph follows me around like I'm the second coming. He'd do just about anything I asked without question.

He brandishes an empty 7-Eleven cup like a trophy. "Mission accomplished."

"You poured a drink on her?"

"Cherry slushy," he beams.

"Dude. That may have been taking it a little too far."

"You *said*—"

"I said wreck her dress, I didn't say to pour a drink on her!"

"Well, what did you want me to do? She was already wearing it! It was this or a mud pie."

I don't know what I expected him to do. It's just that I can't stop picturing Ava the way she looked outside the library that day—anxious, timid, about to burst into tears—and now I'm picturing her like that but with slushy all over her, and I'm pretty sure that makes me an asshole.

But she wants out of the Prom Bowl. And thanks to me, the bids on her will be way low. I finger the stack of twenties, saved up from odd jobs around the neighborhood, that I carefully paper clipped together and tucked into my breast pocket in anticipation of tonight. It's win-win. I'll take her to prom, and I'll make it absolutely perfect. She won't even remember tonight after I'm done.

Murph is watching me anxiously, so I knock my knuckles against his shoulder. "It's good, man."

He grins, his pride restored, and scampers off toward the freshman section.

I turn my focus to the gym floor. It always looks so much smaller from up here. Our gym is set up with the bleachers on an upper balcony ringing the court, so spectators can look down on the basketball or volleyball games. Tonight, though, the basketball hoops have been folded up into the gridwork of the ceiling, and alternating purple and gold streamers run from the bottom of the scoreboard to the walls. Down below us, a long red carpet winds from the girls' locker room all the way around a full lap of the gym.

As I take everything in, the lights start to dim over the bleachers. The voices around me get louder. A couple of people even whistle, like they think maybe they can get the girls out here sooner if they call them like dogs. Just before the lights fade all the way, Cody slips into the empty space beside me.

"Where've you been?" I ask him.

"Setting up. The DJ was having electrical problems."

"You know how to solve electrical problems?"

He grins. "She needed an extra power strip."

"Ah."

"So I stole one from AP Euro History."

"The mark of a true professional."

He shushes me.

The music kicks in. It's some candy-pop thing from the early part of this century. I know I've heard it before, probably during halftime at away games or something. Beside me, I can feel Cody getting caught up in the rhythm, head-bobbing along with the beat. Lucky son of a bitch. Cody doesn't have to worry about scraping money together for the girl he likes. He can just sit back and enjoy the show.

Caity Pierce appears first in the locker room doorway. She stalks like a cheetah in black high-heeled shoes and a red dress with such a low neckline that I can tell she's not wearing a bra. Behind her comes Denise Mellibosky in a short black dress with a section cut out around the middle to expose her stomach and lower back, followed by Sarah Leavett in a fitted dress the same color as her pale skin. I actually think she's naked for a second.

Cody whistles and stamps his feet.

Amy Spicoli, in a shiny blue skintight dress that laces together all the way down the back, stops and blows a kiss into the bleachers. Charlotte Ramsey grips her skirt when she's halfway around the gym and shimmies it up her leg, teasingly. Joanna York is in a white dress that has no back at all, except for at the very bottom, where it literally contours to each of her butt cheeks.

Jesus. I need a shower.

Hannah Bauman gives me a break by coming out in a floor-length pink dress. She's followed by Solstice Downing, who's just cute in a sundress with daisies on it. I like Solstice, even though she kind of has a reputation; that reputation is probably what secured her spot in the Prom Bowl. But just because a girl's been around doesn't mean she's not nice. I mean, if anything, it means she *is* nice.

Maria Baker.

Kylie Richards.

Elizabeth Kepler.

I'm counting now.

Marlee Wheeler, wobbling a little on stilettos that put her a head above anybody else out there. *Twelve.* Olivia Merchant,

Cody's date tonight, in a bright orange number that fans out when she twirls. Cody howls. *Thirteen.*

Emily Hickman. The door swings shut behind her.

Fourteen.

Cody sits forward. "Where is she?"

Took the words right out of my mouth.

He turns to me. "Did you do something?"

I play dumb. "What do you mean?"

"Why isn't the Wild Card out there?"

"She has a name, dude."

"Okay, so?"

"So how should I know where she is?" I feel like I'm swallowing rocks. Did Ava pull herself out of the show because of what I did? How upset is she? I should never have done this. I bet I humiliated her. Do I tell her it was me? She'll be mad, but at least she'll know she wasn't being picked on. I don't want her to think people see her as a joke. But I'm also trying to get this girl to like me!

Maybe she'll understand.

I don't know. Maybe I just shouldn't say anything.

Cody smacks my arm. "Here we go."

"Huh?"

"Fashionably late, I guess."

I look up.

Holy shit, is that Ava?

Jesus, I thought she wasn't going to try.

Is it possible she thinks this is *not* trying? Her hair is swept into a messy pile at the top of her head, and her dress is a rich purple strappy thing that leaves her shoulders bare and just skims the tops of her breasts. Sequins wind from her right shoulder to her hip in feathery patterns, catching the light and pulling my attention to all the places the dress clings. Did she just throw this together without thought or effort? And if so, how are we going to get through three events without someone else noticing her?

She doesn't stalk. She doesn't twirl. She doesn't hike up her skirt and flash some leg. She simply walks the length of the carpet and takes her place in line beside Emily. She gives a little wave as she stops. She's facing the other side of the bleachers. She's facing away from me.

Who is she waving to?

Was that just showmanship?

Does she have a date tonight?

Wait, what happened with the slushy?

As the girls file out and the lights come up, I get to my feet and push my way through the crowd. I find Murph in between two freshman cheerleaders, an arm around each of their shoulders. He's whispering in one girl's ear, making her giggle and leaving the other looking annoyed. I clear my throat.

Murph looks up.

I glare at him and he raises both palms in defense. "I don't know what to tell you, man."

"Because, like, there was *nothing* wrong with that dress." Not one damn thing wrong with that dress.

"She wasn't wearing that dress!"

"What?"

"Nah, dude, she was wearing a totally different dress. A butt-ugly dress!" The girls giggle. "She must have, like, changed."

"And you didn't think maybe her ugly dress was what she wore on the way over?"

"All the other girls were already in fancy dresses. I watched through the window."

I sigh. "Of course you did."

"Nobody was changing, man. I don't even know where she got that dress. She must have gone back home for it or something."

"Mark?"

I turn. Ava's peeking up over the concrete wall that divides the bleachers from the stairs that lead down to the court.

"Did you need something?" Cody appears at my elbow. His tone isn't unfriendly, but he's not exactly inviting her to join us either. I see the moment when Ava places him as the guy who was a dick to her at the football game.

"Good show," I tell her. There's so much else I want to say—that she's beautiful in that dress, that she should only ever wear that dress, that *what the hell is she thinking* wearing that dress, and doesn't she realize that every guy here is looking at her and mentally analyzing his budget and my wad of twenties is feeling pretty damn worthless right now? But I can't find the words for any of it.

"Thanks." She smiles, barely. She's still watching Cody.

"Yeah," Cody inserts himself into the conversation. "Cute dress."

She runs her hands over her stomach. "It isn't mine. Mine, um, got dirty. I had to borrow one from Ms. Loren."

Well that explains it. "Bad luck," I say.

"Good luck, really. My other dress was a piece of crap."

Cody's hand is on my arm. "C'mon, let's go hook up with Liv. She's got the vodka."

"You go on ahead. I want to talk to Ava a minute."

She blushes, and suddenly I want to grab her and kiss her.

Cody stares. "Is something going on with you guys?"

I don't answer. Ava bites her lip and stares at the floor.

"Whatever." He brushes past me and jogs down the stairs.

Ava waits until he's around the corner, out of earshot. "*Is* something going on with us?"

"What do you think?"

She frowns. "Are you testing me or something?"

"What? No! I meant like . . . do you *want* there to be something going on with us?"

"Do *you*?"

"I asked first."

"I'm pretty sure I did."

"I . . . huh."

She cracks a smile. "You really think I was good tonight?"

"The truth?"

"Of course."

"I really think you're going to get a lot of bids tonight." I stuff my hands in my pockets to prevent myself from running my fingers across the bills I have stashed in my shirt.

Ava

Is Mark avoiding answering the question?

I ask myself this over and over as he leads me around the gym, and if I'm honest, it does get in the way of my enjoying the dance. If he wanted something to happen, wouldn't he say so? He's Quarterback Mark Palmer, it's not as if he doesn't know how to ask for what he wants.

He's not asking for me.

I don't get it. I thought our date went well. I even thought he might ask me to homecoming. Then, when he didn't, I thought maybe Dad told the players they weren't allowed to bring dates so they could focus on the game, which is the kind of freaky controlling thing Dad does to his players. But Sean's here with some girl who picked him up in her electric blue Infiniti. So it's not a football thing.

I guess I was wrong. I guess Mark isn't that into me.

I pull away after our third dance in a row. Better to be the one walking away than the one left behind. "I need to go get a drink," I tell him.

"Do you want me to come with you?" His hand finds the small of my back and then dips slightly lower.

"No." I step away quickly. Too quickly, I realize, as I take in his wounded expression. "I mean, I'm fine. Stay here and dance."

I make my way through the mass of bodies to the bright light and relative cool of the bathroom, which is, thankfully, empty. I stand back and take in my reflection. There's no mirror in the costume closet, so I haven't had a chance to see myself in this dress. The fit is tight—tighter than anything I've ever worn—so I assumed I would look like I'd been stuffed into it.

I was wrong.

I've never seen a dress that fits me like this, and it sort of feels like a fairy godmother situation. If I didn't know better, I'd say it was tailor-made for me. Of course it wasn't, it was just pulled out of a closet of hand-me-downs, which means there are dresses out in the wild that could look like this on me.

I look beautiful.

I look sexy.

Anyone can find the perfect dress. It's just a matter of knowing where to look. My mother used to say that. She'd say it in department stores as she swept through like a force of nature, plucking garments off their racks with one hand, towing me behind her with the other. She'd say it in my bedroom, laying mail-order discoveries out on my bed for me to try on. At some point, though, I had decided she was wrong. *Some people* could find the perfect dress. Thin people could, and tall people could, and curvy people whose curves were in exactly the right places could, and even short people could if they tried hard. But I'd never even come close to finding my perfect dress, with perhaps the exception of the yellow one my mother had bought for me. Not that I'm ever going to wear that one again.

The door bangs open behind me. Three girls come in, their heads bent together to create their own proprietary universe of gossip and friendship. ". . . isn't even *here* tonight, she was too embarrassed to show her face," one of them is saying.

"But, like, can it kill you?" her friend asks, in a hushed tone.

"I think it can, if you don't get it treated. Can I borrow your lipstick?"

"Hey, you're from the fashion show," says the third girl.

It takes me a minute too long to realize she's talking to me, and by the time I figure it out the silence has become awkward. I wish I could bolt myself in a stall and wait for them to leave. "Yeah. Um, yes. I'm Ava. That's me."

"You were *so good*!" The girl flings her arms around me. I stagger back a step under her weight. "Wow. I mean, you were just *so* good."

"She was just walking, Cassie, keep it in your pants." The first girl shakes her head. Blonde curls are spilling out of her updo. "I'm Jess. Sorry about her. You really were good, though. It's nice to have someone out there repping for the real girls, for once. Prom Bowl's always so twiggy."

None of these three could realistically be called twiggy. Jess, easily the biggest of the three, is probably a good twenty pounds heavier than I am.

"Are you seniors too?"

"We're sophomores. You know Cassie. This is Sam."

Sam, sandy-haired and tall, flashes crooked teeth at me.

"We think it's so cool you're in the Prom Bowl," Cassie says.

"You do?"

"Yeah, I mean, we came to this thing last year and every girl out there was five-foot-seven, a hundred and ten pounds, white—"

"At least they've got a black girl this year," Jess says.

"Kylie was a given, though," Cassie says dismissively.

"You thought Laura was a given."

"Kylie doesn't spread *deadly diseases*."

"Anyway."

"Anyway, the point is, it's easy to start feeling like guys only want to bring one type of girl to prom. And we're not that type."

"It's just nice to see somebody different in the mix, is what she's saying," Jess says.

I sort of feel like I should be offended. They're pointing out the exact thing I've been worrying about all night—that I don't fit in with the other girls in the Bowl, that I'm not pretty like they are and that other people have noticed—but for some reason, I'm actually kind of proud. Maybe me being part of Prom Bowl is actually doing someone some good. And if that's true, maybe it's okay that I went out there in this dress tonight, that Mark got to see me looking sexy instead of gross in the Chrome Cricket dress. Maybe it's okay if I make it through to the second round. I can always get eliminated there, and in the meantime, these girls got to see someone other than a cookie-cutter contestant do well.

"Ava! Thank *fucking God*!"

All four of us jump.

Charlotte barrels into the bathroom like a runaway train. "Where the hell have you been? I've looked literally everywhere for you."

"What's wrong? Are you okay?"

"We have to go home."

"Why? What's going on?"

She waves her phone at me. "My mom just texted. She knows about the credit card."

I groan. "I told you that was a bad idea."

"Yeah, well, she's pissed off, like, to the ground. I need to get back there before she builds up a head of steam about it."

"Actually, I kind of think I'm not ready to go yet."

She stares. "Seriously? You're going to pull this shit on me? She is going to *literally* kill me."

"She's not going to *literally* kill you," Cassie speaks up.

Charlotte stares. "Who the fuck are you?"

"I can take you home, Ava," Jess says.

"Jess can take me home," I parrot.

"Who the fuck is Jess?"

I make an exhibit-A gesture.

Charlotte throws up her hands like a diva, and for the first time I wonder whether maybe she's been drinking. "Fine. Whatever."

"Are you sure you're okay to drive?"

"I'm *fine*."

"Because I bet my dad would come pick you up. You know, that whole parent thing about how if people have been drinking and you need a ride, no questions asked?"

"I haven't been drinking, Ava, I'm *freaking out*, okay? Whatever. Fuck. Stay with your friends."

Charlotte storms out. She shoves at the door as she's leaving, like she wants to slam it, but the pneumatic hinges kill the effect and the door glides closed, way too cool for Charlotte.

Jess, Cassie, and Sam all look at me.

I am Senior Ava Vanguard, Prom Bowl Knockout.

"Let's dance," I say.

PATTERSON HIGH PROM BOWL

Private

Cody Spencer

Posted 2 min ago

The results are in! Bidding is closed, and the offers have been recorded. You may have already seen this list on the public Prom Bowl event page, but in case you haven't, here are the results. The number you see by your name is the highest bid you've received so far, so anyone wanting to bid on you next round will have to top that amount. As of one week from now, the girls with the five lowest bids will be removed from this group and from the competition—sorry, ladies!

Joanna York—$20
Emily Hickman—$20
Elizabeth Kepler—$40
Sarah Leavett—$50
Olivia Merchant—$50
Hannah Bauman—$80
Amy Spicoli—$100
Ava Vanguard—$120
Denise Mellibosky—$120
Charlotte Ramsey—$120
Kylie Richards—$150
Maria Baker—$170
Solstice Downing—$180
Marlee Wheeler—$200
Caity Pierce—$200

Like • Reply

Marlee Wheeler, Maria Baker, and 4 others like this

Amy Spicoli:
Sorry **Joanna Emily Elizabeth Olivia Sarah** :(:(
Posted 2 min ago • **Like** • **Reply**

Mark Palmer
$1,620 raised for prom so far—keep up the good work!

MEMBERS
Cody Spencer
Mark Palmer
Caity Pierce
Amy Spicoli
Sarah Leavett
Marlee Wheeler
Olivia Merchant
Solstice Downing
Joanna York
Denise Mellibosky
Elizabeth Kepler
Maria Baker
Charlotte Ramsey
Emily Hickman
Hannah Bauman
Kylie Richards
Wild Card: Ava Vanguard

7

Mark

I've got her.

I stayed up all night after the homecoming dance refreshing my Internet browser, watching the bidding on the Prom Bowl page. Cody had been talking all through the dance about stopping on the way home for a four-pack of Monsters so he could stay up and manage the bids, and I took the hint and did the same. At four in the morning, I sent him a text raising the bid on Ava from a hundred dollars to one twenty. It's more money than I have, but I still have until spring to get it together.

Ava's not out of the next round. But for now, at least, she's mine.

Not that she knows it. Stupid anonymous bidding system.

I spot her on the opposite side of the lawn at Luther Hills Senior Center, raking leaves into a neat pile. It's the first time I've seen her at a Key Club event—the weekly meetings conflict with football practice, so I can't go to them—and it's a pleasant surprise. Really, it shouldn't be so surprising. Tons of seniors join Key Club when the last-minute résumé panic hits. Today's crowd is mostly juniors, though, because it's the last ACT testing weekend until December, and if you want to do a retake and boost your score before college application deadlines, now is the time.

We break for lunch after a couple of hours of raking. Ava sits down right where she is under one of the oak trees that's been shedding all over the lawn and pulls a brown bag and a book out of her backpack.

Okay then. I grab my own lunch and go over to her. "Hey."

"Hey."

"Do you mind if I join you?" I ask as I drop down beside her.

She laughs. "Looks like you already are."

"But you were going to say yes, right?"

"Maybe."

"You so were, don't lie."

"Okay, okay."

The double-knotted handles of the grocery bag containing my lunch are too hard to break into, so I rip the plastic open at the bottom instead. Tupperware containers spill out all around me.

"What's for lunch?" Ava peels a banana.

I peek into the first container. Suspicions confirmed. "Pumpkin."

"What?"

"My mom's doing the seasonal food trend thing." I angle my container toward Ava and she peeks in at my two slices of pumpkin bread. "She works at a restaurant and she's always trying to pitch her boss new menu ideas."

"So this could actually end up on a menu?"

"Nah, probably not. They listen to her, but they don't, y'know, *listen* to her."

"What else did she make?"

I check. "Salad with pumpkin seeds, and . . . I don't know what these are."

"Tartlets!"

"Do you want one?"

"You sure?"

"I've got five, I'll be fine."

Ava accepts a tartlet and pops it into her mouth whole.

"So," I say.

"So?"

"So you made the top ten."

"Oh. Yeah."

"Didn't go the way you planned."

She shrugs. "Yeah. It was the dress."

I nudge her shoulder. "It wasn't just the dress."

She makes a study of her banana and doesn't answer.

"You saw your bid, right?"

"I don't know who would bid a hundred and twenty dollars on me."

I want to tell her. I so want to tell her. "Someone who saw how great you looked that night."

"Uh-huh."

"I know you wanted to be eliminated, but, like, c'mon. It's kind of flattering, right?"

She raises her eyebrows. "Flattering?"

Uh oh. "Not flattering?"

"I mean, it's kind of creepy. Someone wants to pay a hundred and twenty dollars for me based on what? How I looked in a dress? A dress that isn't even mine?"

"You looked great in it."

"That's so not the point. I don't know who this person is. He doesn't know who *I* am. I don't know, maybe the rest of you think this stuff is normal because you've all known each other for years, but I'm new here. I don't know anybody. Nobody knows me."

"Maybe somebody wants to get to know you."

"So sit next to me in class. Or—"

"Or at lunch?"

"Exactly."

I wait.

She darts her head up to meet my eyes. "Wait, did you—?"

"Bidding's anonymous," I tell her, all business. "I'm not allowed to reveal what I may or may not have bid on anyone."

"You *did*! I thought you didn't like me!"

"I thought we established we had a thing between us."

"Yeah, no, you never really gave me a definite answer on that. *And* you were acting all weird on homecoming night."

"Weird how?"

"Distant."

"Preoccupied, I guess." I don't want to tell her I was worrying I might not be able to afford her. That isn't sexy.

"So . . . so you like me." She says the words carefully, like she's experimenting with a dangerous flavor. Taking it slow. Afraid of being burned.

"Ava," I say, "would you like to go to prom with me?"

She laughs. "Do I have a choice?"

"Yes." I take her hand. I'm not laughing. "You do."

"If . . . if I say no?"

"Then I'll pay my bid to the Prom Bowl fund and that will be that."

"You'll let me go."

"You don't belong to me."

"Did you outbid someone else? Or did you just start the bidding at one twenty?"

"At least one other person."

"Then they could still win, right? How can I promise to go to the prom with you?"

"Don't promise. Just . . . would you like to?"

She bites her lip and looks down. She literally can't look me in the eye, poor kid.

"Yeah," she says. "Yes. I would. Thank you."

Yes. She would. I fall backward into the pile of leaves, scattering them, and throw my arms above my head in triumph. She wants me. I want her. It's *so* on.

Ava squawks. "I spent all morning on that!"

I reach up and grab her arm, pulling her down with me. "I'll help you fix it." I bury my fingers in her hair, and my hands crunch the leaves tangled there as I pull her close and kiss her.

She's not a good kisser. She's rigid in my arms, and she sucks her lips in. She's inexperienced. I rub my thumb behind her ear. It's fine. We can take it slow. We have plenty of time.

I only have to make sure no one else bids on her. That's all.

Ava

I fall back behind Charlotte as we enter the Steak 'n' Shake. I hope all the other girls are here already. I want to take the last available seat. That way, no one will be able to question why I sat where I did. They'll see I had no options. I tug on the hem of my skirt in case it's riding up in the back. Charlotte's wearing jeans and a tank top. I should have worn jeans. Who dresses up for Steak 'n' Shake? Someone who's trying too hard, that's who.

"You have to come hang out with everybody," Charlotte had said. "You have to get to know the other girls. You don't want people to think you're some weirdo loner, right?"

First Dad and now her. Why is it so freaky to like being alone? This is the kind of thing I used to talk to my mom about, when I talked to her. Sean and Dad were the social addicts. Mom was like me—happy to stay at home. You know. Until she wasn't.

I did what Charlotte wanted, in the end, because going along with the Charlotte Express is easier than arguing. Anyway, it's just dinner. I can handle dinner. I eat dinner all the time!

I have *got* to relax.

The girls have pulled a few tables together along the far wall of the restaurant to make one long one. Charlotte blows past the hostess, calling out "Hey guys!" loudly enough that other diners look up from their bowls of chili.

"Hey Char." This from a redheaded girl with piercings all the way up the outside of her ear. I wonder if she knows how much Charlotte hates nicknames.

"Hey Denise," Charlotte says. "This is my cousin Ava."

"The Wild Card," Denise nods. "You were good at the runway show."

"Thanks."

"The Wild Card usually doesn't make it through the first round. Everyone's talking about you."

"Oh. They are?"

Denise laughs. "Don't look so concerned, Wild Card. Nothing bad. Well, nothing *too* bad."

"Denise, can you stop trying to turn dinner into a CW show, please?" says the girl at the end of the table. She motions to the empty seat beside her. "Sit, Ava."

I sit.

"I'm Solstice." She waves, which is weird since she's right next to me, but kind of endearing. "You're new, right? How are you liking Patterson?"

"It's crazy that she's in Prom Bowl, isn't it?" Charlotte cuts in before I have a chance to answer. "Has a new girl ever been picked before?"

"She's dating Mark Palmer, though," says a blonde girl, picking a shred out of a bowl of coleslaw.

"No she isn't," Charlotte scoffs.

"They were making out at the Key Club thing. Wil saw them."

Charlotte whips her head around. "You were?"

"No, I . . . I don't know. We were talking."

"Did he kiss you?" someone demands.

"Um, do I know you?"

"I'm Amy. Did Mark kiss you?"

I take a second to relive the way he pressed me between his body and the leaves, the smell of fall and something spicy when he kissed me, and the joy of that moment. I don't want to share it with this girl.

"Write up a full incident report and submit it to the relationship verification committee," Solstice says. "Then we'll let you know whether you're officially dating or not."

Most of the others laugh. I exhale and give Solstice a grateful smile; I'm off the hook for now. "I'll get right on that."

Amy frowns and stabs her salad hard with her fork.

"But that's probably why she's doing well in the Bowl," says the blonde girl. "He's probably got the whole football team bidding for her."

Denise shakes her head. "Doesn't make sense. If Mark likes her, he'll be pulling for her to get eliminated early so he can buy her at a lower price."

"He wouldn't do that," I speak up.

She raises an eyebrow. "So Marlee's right? He's campaigning for you?"

"No!"

"Because that's pretty sketch, Wild Card."

My face is hot. I grip my sweating glass of water to wet my hand and press the condensation into my cheeks. "Nobody's campaigning for me. I don't even—I was hoping to get eliminated last round."

"What?" Amy squeals.

Denise sits back in her chair and folds her arms across her chest like she's watching *Jerry Springer*.

"Ava!" Charlotte bounces in her chair a little. "How many times do I have to explain it to you? This contest is really important. It determines who you spend your senior prom with! And the winner's going to be prom queen!"

Being prom queen sounds categorically awful to me. I'm pretty sure whoever receives the crown has to dance with their date in front of the entire school. I might actually die.

"Not everybody wants to be prom queen, Charlotte," Solstice says.

"*Of course* everybody wants to be prom queen!"

"Samuel L. Jackson doesn't want to be prom queen. Eminem doesn't want to be prom queen."

"Every *girl*."

"Jane Goodall."

"Who?" Charlotte looks confused. Denise and a few of the other girls laugh. Point Solstice.

"Anyway," I say as the laughter dies down, "I don't want to be bid on. I want a say in who I go to prom with." I want to go with Mark, but they don't need to know that.

"You're still going to get bids," Marlee points out, rearranging her coleslaw. "Even if you were already out, you'd have been bought."

"Yeah, but . . . I don't know. Maybe the guys who pay less expect less." Maybe I can just dance with the guy once or twice and then do my own thing the rest of the night.

"Definitely true," Solstice agrees.

"We're the lucky ones," says a girl at the other end of the table. "I mean, yeah, the whole thing's kind of dumb, but at least we don't have to worry about getting dates."

"Who's got your high bid right now?" Charlotte's friend, Kylie, asks me.

"Aren't the bids anonymous?"

A chorus of laughter runs down the length of the table.

"What's funny?"

"It's anonymous like who's sleeping with who is a secret," Solstice says. "Like, everyone swears they aren't going to tell, and then everyone does anyway."

"Although it might be faster to say who some people *aren't* sleeping with," a girl a few seats down says. "Be a shorter list."

Solstice rolls her eyes. "Nice one, Caity. I like how your jokes match your boots."

Caity frowns, confused.

"Last year's," Solstice supplies.

This time I join in the laughter.

"I'm trying to get Giovanni or Alex or someone to buy me cheap so I can just go with Zoe," Denise says. "Sucks that girls aren't allowed to bid."

"Cameron's going to bid on me," Caity informs us.

"Really? How do you know?" Kylie asks.

"He told me."

"What if he gets outbid?" Denise asks.

"He's been saving for months. Packing lunches instead of eating off campus, and no new video games all year."

"Wow."

"I know, right?"

I have to admit, there's a part of me—a little part, a part I don't respect very much, but it is there—that wonders whether Mark would do something like that for me. Whether any boy would.

The server comes by with a grilled cheese sandwich for Denise and a strawberry shake for Solstice. "Anything else for you ladies?"

"Oh. No thank you," I say.

"Watching your figure?" Denise gives me a shrewd look.

I feel like I'm going to burn up on the spot. "Just not hungry."

"Want this?" Marlee tips her coleslaw at me. "I'm done."

"No thanks." *Stop staring, stop staring, stop staring.* I know what they're all thinking—that I'm too fat, that it doesn't make sense for me to be in the second round of Prom Bowl, that nobody is going to bid on me and there won't be as much money for prom as there would have been if one of the prettier girls had made it through instead of me. That I'm ruining everything.

"You're in my Chem class, right?" Solstice asks.

Or that. "Um, yes."

"Have you done the lab yet?"

"The write-up? Yeah. I think my conclusion is wrong."

"Oh my God," Charlotte interrupts. "I can't even *do* the write-up because I didn't get a result when I did the experiment. My compound just sat there like it was dead. I'm so going to fail."

"You can still do the write-up," Solstice says. "You just write up the experiment and put that the result was inconclusive."

Charlotte grabs her arm. "Can I read yours, Solstice, please?"

"Don't let her, Sol," Denise instructs.

"Stay out of it, Denise!"

"The teacher's kind of a hardass, isn't he?" I venture.

"Larson? The worst." Marlee leans in. "A few years ago there was a girl who was all set to go to Yale on scholarship until Larson flunked her. Now she works at Burger Barn."

"That didn't happen," Denise rolls her eyes.

"My cousin's friend went to prom with the girl!"

"Was she in the Prom Bowl?" I ask.

"Not after she failed Physics and lost her scholarship. She had to drop out."

"Bullshit," Denise declares.

"I swear. It happened."

Solstice catches my gaze, rolls her eyes, and offers me her straw. I take a sip of milkshake.

I guess that's one way out of Prom Bowl.

PATTERSON HIGH PROM BOWL

Private

Cody Spencer

Posted 5 min ago

Prom Bowl Talent Contest
November 1, 7 pm-9 pm
Paterson High Auditorium

ROUND TWO—DING!
Congratulations, girls, you've made it past the first round. You're all gorgeous and you totally earned it. BUT! There is more to life than just looks! Now's your chance to show us what else you have to offer. After all, a guy wants a well-rounded prom date with a knack for entertainment. So bring your hottest skills and be prepared to entertain!

Like • Reply

Solstice Downing and 2 others like this

Denise Mellibosky

Can someone give me a ride to this?

Posted 1 min ago • **Like • Reply**

Solstice Downing

I got you girl!

Posted 30 sec ago • **Like • Reply**

Denise Mellibosky

Thanks. <3

Posted 2 sec ago • **Like • Reply**

MEMBERS

Cody Spencer
Mark Palmer
Caity Pierce
Amy Spicoli
Marlee Wheeler
Solstice Downing
Denise Mellibosky
Maria Baker
Charlotte Ramsey
Hannah Bauman
Kylie Richards
Wild Card: Ava Vanguard

8

Ava

I don't have any talent.

All right. That isn't strictly true. I'm pretty good at literary analysis, I can knit a sock, and I do just as neat a job painting the nails on my right hand as on my left hand. I can do a five-thousand-piece puzzle that's nothing but ocean and sky in the span of a weekend. What I don't have is a *showable* talent. It's not like I can get up onstage and paint my nails. I'm screwed here.

Which is actually kind of perfect.

This isn't like the fashion show. No one's going to haul me into a closet and slap a borrowed talent on me at the last minute. And, unlike the fashion show, I can actually try here. Because even if I do my level best, it's not going to get me anywhere. There is no way I survive this round.

I'm out of the Prom Bowl, Mark's bid wins, we go to prom together, game over.

I'm going to sing.

That ought to scare everyone.

I've borrowed the backing track CD from Sean's karaoke

machine, and tonight I will be performing "I Will Always Love You" by Whitney Houston, the bane of karaoke singers everywhere. You have to have a powerful voice to perform this song, to hit those high notes after the key change. You have to belt. And the thing is that nobody really likes the song, but everyone loves those few notes, so if I butcher that part, it really doesn't matter how I sound the rest of the time.

And there's no way I can hit those high notes.

"Do you think people will laugh?" Solstice asks me backstage.

"Of course they won't laugh at you." I do a couple of mouth stretches, opening wide and then scrunching up small. This may or may not be a real thing singers do to warm up. Doesn't matter.

"Ava, I'm doing stand-up comedy!"

"Oh! Sorry. Scratch that. Yes. They will totally laugh."

"Really, you think so?"

"Of course. You're hilarious." Sol and I have been hanging out since Steak 'n' Shake night. She hasn't been to my house yet, but I've been to hers. I don't think her parents even want to venture a guess as to what decade they're in. They've got incense burning in every room, AC/DC on the stereo, and this amazing floral wallpaper that looks like something out of a movie. No wonder Sol is so good at rolling with things.

Caity Pierce walks by on her hands and falls forward into a graceful walkover. On the far side of the room, Kylie Richards is sitting in a wide split with her arms over her head while Denise Mellibosky tunes her guitar.

Charlotte clacks across the room in heels so high I'm amazed she isn't pitching forward. She's wearing sheer tights with torn short shorts and a low-cut tank top. "I'm up first, Ava!"

"Yeah?"

"You'll watch, right?"

"I'll be in the wings," I promise her.

She runs off to take the stage.

Solstice watches her go. "What's her talent, exactly?"

"I'm not sure."

"I thought you two were friends."

"She's my cousin."

"So, not friends?"

"I don't know. It's complicated. We didn't talk about what we were going to do in the show."

"Hmm."

"Oh, come on, what?"

"I've just never known Charlotte Ramsey to have any particular talent."

I throw my hoodie at her. "Be nice."

"I'm not being mean."

"You're not being *nice*."

"I'm just asking a question."

"Well, I don't know. Come on, come watch with me."

We slip between two curtains, upstage of where Charlotte is standing. Amy Spicoli is in the wings too, running her hands over her bare stomach where it's exposed by her cheerleading uniform.

"Is cheerleading a talent?" Solstice whispers in my ear.

I shrug. "Don't see why not."

Onstage, Charlotte takes the mic off its stand. "Looks like someone left a pole on stage for me!" she says. "Trying to tell me something, Cody?"

Someone hoots.

Charlotte holds the mic stand in one hand and slides down slowly. "Wow. It's so *dirty* down here."

Howls from the audience.

"I have a confession to make." She straightens up and bites her fingernail. The fake shyness is so transparent that I'm embarrassed for her, but clearly she isn't embarrassed for herself. "I'm not so great at keeping things clean."

Amy Spicoli shakes her head and walks off, pushing past us. I guess she's seen enough and I don't really blame her. This is ridiculous.

"Especially," Charlotte adds, "in my bedroom."

That earns her an actual round of applause. Seriously? This counts as a talent?

"I thought it would only be right to bring it up," Charlotte says. "If anyone's thinking of bidding on me, you should know what you're getting into."

"Charlotte Ramsey likes it dirty!" someone shouts, and everyone laughs.

"They think that's funny?" I hiss in Solstice's ear. "She didn't even make a joke. It's just a double entendre. It's barely even that."

"They're laughing, though."

"They're laughing *at* her. They're calling her a slut."

"She's calling herself that."

"Well yeah. It still isn't funny."

"But this is the kind of joke people want to hear. They're all going to vote for her."

"What, you think people are going to compare you to her? That's not going to happen. You two are completely different."

"Yeah?"

"I mean, you actually tell *jokes*, for one thing."

She cracks a smile. "You're right."

"I know I am."

Charlotte comes offstage to raucous cheers. "Ava! How'd I do?"

"Um, awesome."

"Funny, right?"

Cody's back onstage, speaking into the microphone. His voice sounds like it's coming from somewhere way up in the curtain rigging. "Up next with a little more humor for you—Solstice Downing!"

Solstice grips my arm.

I nudge her. "Get out there. You got this."

"Go Solstice!" Charlotte whisper-cheers.

Sol gives me a terrified look and steps out onto the stage. Charlotte marched toward the microphone like it was her personal property. Sol looks more like she's afraid it's going to lunge at her.

"Is she okay?" Charlotte asks.

"Yeah. Nervous. About following you."

"I was that good, really?"

"I think you'll definitely get a lot of votes," I say dryly.

She makes a little squee face and runs off toward the greenroom.

Solstice is fussing with the height of the mic. "Hey everybody," she says, too close, and jumps back, startled by the reverb effect of her own voice.

"Can't hear you!" some jackass yells.

"I speak one language," Solstice says, "and that's English. I don't even take a language credit, actually, because my parents are hippies and thought it was really important for me to learn macramé. Which is great for decorating their house, but doesn't do me much good when we travel. Last summer I was in Italy, and we decided to go to the opera, and at that time the only show we could get tickets for was this German thing—"

"Tell some *jokes*!"

"I'm getting there. The Italian opera house is this big, round theater, and of course it's not air-conditioned. Air-conditioning is sort of like ice cubes for your drinks in that they don't really bother with it in Europe. We Americans must just really hate being hot or something. So anyway, I'm at the opera—"

"Can't *heeeeeaaar* you!"

I watch Solstice close her eyes, take one deep breath in, exhale. Then she yanks the mic off the stand.

"You can't hear me? Really?" The shakiness is gone from her voice. She sounds pissed. "Can you actually not hear me? Who is that? You want to stand up?"

She waits. Apparently the heckler does not want to stand up.

"Is anyone having trouble hearing me now? Because I'd hate for you to miss out. Tell you what, by a show of hands—do you think you'd hear me any better if I took my top off?"

Wait, *what*?

Pandemonium. The show of hands is entirely unnecessary. Solstice has brought the house down. And as I stand there staring at her, she rips her T-shirt over her head, throws it into the crowd like some kind of rock star, and stands there under the stage lights in her pink and teal bra.

I can't believe it. I can't believe she let a heckler push her that far.

Solstice takes an elaborate bow, dripping so much sarcasm that the next person up is liable to slip in it, replaces the mic, and walks offstage.

"Solstice!" I yell.

She ignores me.

Behind me, I can hear Cody reining in the crowd. "Okay everyone, I've been asked to remind the girls to keep the show family-friendly."

A chorus of boos.

I catch Solstice's arm as she storms past. "Hey. Hey!"

"What?"

"What happened out there?"

"Do you mind if we talk about this somewhere else? I kind of want to get dressed."

I hurry to keep up with her. "What the hell *was* that?"

"Hey, it worked, right?" She pushes into the greenroom.

I catch the swinging door before it smacks me in the face and follow her. "You totally played into their shit, Sol. I thought we agreed we weren't going to let them manipulate us."

"This isn't my shirt. . . ."

"Solstice!"

She turns on me. "Ava, seriously? Stop it. We've been playing into their shit since the beginning. They *make* us play into their shit. We're here because we got voted in. They set us up to compete against each other in stupid competitions that are completely transparent."

"What are you talking about?"

"Do you honestly think that fashion show was about who has the best taste in dresses? It was about who looks the hottest. They dressed us up and put us on parade. Now Charlotte's going to get through to round three because she got up on stage and basically promised to fuck any guy who buys her, and I'm probably going to get through because I took my top off."

"Your jokes were funny, Solstice! You didn't have to sell out like this!"

"This is not a funny joke contest, Ava. This isn't a real fucking talent show. If you don't get that, I can't help you."

I'm so pissed off that the next words practically fall out of my mouth. "Do you know what girls are called who take off their clothes for money?"

"Wow. Seriously? Fuck you." She yanks the shirt over her head and storms off, leaving me shaking.

Pep band music starts up from the stage, and I imagine tall, sexy Amy Spicoli shaking the skirt of her immaculate cheerleading uniform. Of course it counts as a talent. That's the most talent anyone's shown today.

I duck into the bathroom to splash some water on my face. I'm not an idiot. I know it's not a real talent show. It's just another occasion for those of us who've been thrown into the Prom Bowl to prove how much we're worth. But I can't believe that Solstice—*Solstice,* who I thought was on my side—went along with it. Has everyone but me lost their minds?

A retching sound echoes from inside one of the toilet stalls.

"Is someone in here?" I turn around.

The sound again, followed by a splatter. I glance under the stall door. Sure enough, someone's heels are pointed toward me.

"Are you okay in there?" I ask. "Want me to get someone?"

The toilet flushes and the door opens. It's Marlee Wheeler, looking pale and sweaty in her loose-fitting leotard. She wipes at her mouth with the back of her hand and brushes by me.

"Marlee? Are you sick?"

"I'm fine."

"If you don't feel well enough to go on—"

"I said I'm *fine,* Wild Card." She pushes the swinging door so hard it slams the wall before easing its way shut, and I stare after her and think about the fit of that leotard and the way she barely touched her coleslaw that night at Steak 'n' Shake.

Are the stakes that high for her? Would she actually make herself sick over this stupid Prom Bowl?

The minute I step out of the bathroom, Cody ambushes me and grabs my arm. "Ava! Jesus, this is no time for a bathroom break, girl. You're on next!"

Immediately I want to run back into the bathroom. "I am?"

"Are you warmed up?"

"I guess." Not that it matters.

"Look." Cody faces me, one hand on each of my shoulders. "I know you're trying to get out of the competition."

"I'm not—"

"Whatever, Palmer already told me."

Mark told him?

He must see the shock on my face. "It's fine, Ava. Honestly, it's a surprise you even made it this far. At this point, you winning would be more suspicious than losing."

"What?" Did he actually just say that?

"So just try and relax. You know. Go out there and do your medium-est. The rest will take care of itself."

"I—"

"You've got *nothing* to worry about," he says, steering me toward the stage. "No one expects you to win this. That's not what you're here for."

He's right. He's probably bidding on Solstice. Or maybe he's bidding on Charlotte. He isn't bidding on me, the girl in the sweater and jeans with the karaoke CD. I'm not the one people are here to see, except as a punch line.

It doesn't matter what I do. The only people who even care what I do are a group of sophomore girls and maybe, possibly, but very likely not, Quarterback Mark Palmer.

Did Cody say that stuff about me being a loser to Mark, I wonder?

Or, God, is it possible that Mark said it to Cody?

This is exactly why I didn't want to be in the Prom Bowl—because I didn't want to be made a fool of. I'm so angry at Cody and his expectant face and his knowing little grin that I can hardly see straight. My rage is burning through any urge to cry.

Which is honestly kind of fucking liberating.

I hand Cody my CD in the paper sleeve. "Track six."

"Go get 'em, Wild Card."

I take the stage.

Here's the thing.

Track six isn't "I Will Always Love You."

"We Are The Champions" is one of about four songs I'm willing to sing along with in the car, usually joined by my brother. It's not about vocal perfection and sailing over high notes. It's about stepping up to the moment. Right now, it's about grabbing the reins away from Cody before he drives us all into the mud.

The music starts, and anyone who was paying attention would recognize it right away, so I don't know if that confirms my theory that no one cares what I do, or if it just means Cody doesn't have access to the CD player anymore. Either way, I'm not allowed to change my song, and someone should be trying to stop me. But they're not.

Power ballad or not, I'm no singer. This isn't a talent I have, and I'm not about to win any prizes for it. But this is a song for a pissed-off girl.

My voice is high and reedy. I think I'm roughly in the neighborhood of the right key at least, but I'm not delusional enough to think this sounds good. Out in the auditorium, I can hear the shuffling and murmuring of hundreds of bored teenagers. I'm not being heckled outright, but it's clear no one gives a damn.

I drop the next line. What am I doing? This song needs confidence. This song needs defiance. This song needs to be bellowed in people's faces, and I am not and have never been a bellower.

God, what am I doing here . . . ?

I'm dizzy. I grip the mic stand and the stage sways like a boat, and the back of my mouth tastes like acid and peanut butter.

I swallow.

I should start singing again, but the song, which I've heard a thousand times in my life, is now unfamiliar. Have I been quiet for two bars or ten? Why does this backing track sound so monotonous?

Peripherally, I can see Cody waving his hands in the wings.

I'm ruining his talent show. I shouldn't care about his talent show. I don't *want* to care.

I don't care.

I close my eyes.

SCREEE! The mic spits feedback and I almost drop it. My eyes fly open. The stage lights have gone out. I'm alone in the dark, and the confusing backing track of my song has been silenced.

A power outage?

Confused, frustrated voices rise from the audience. The noise starts to swell. I tap the mic with two fingers and get nothing, nothing but the soft pad of my skin on mesh.

A *boooo!* comes from the crowd and spurs another, and I thank God no one can see me turning red. This must be how Sol felt when her act went wrong. It's awful. How could I have been so horrible to her? This so-called talent show backed my best friend into a corner and I blamed her for fighting her way out of it.

I could leave the stage right now and no one would care.

But no. Fuck all these people for making Sol feel like she wasn't good enough without debauching her own act. For making me feel like I'm not good enough to even be in the second round. And suddenly whether or not I *am* worthy of this stupid competition isn't the point. I'm in it, and I'm gonna fight, and they all have to sit there and fucking listen because they're the ones who put me here. I'm not going to just walk off the stage in the middle of my song and prove them right. I owe it to Sol. I owe it to *myself*.

I take a deep breath and find my voice for the next lines of my song.

It comes out louder than I'm expecting. I breathe and lean into it. I belt it out.

There's no noise around me anymore. There are no voices. There's me and the darkness and the song. Cody and his flapping hands, they don't matter. I am singing this song the way I sing it in the shower when no one's home—full voice, loud and confident. I *am* the champion. I pull my way through the second verse, hand over hand, note over note. The tremor is gone from my voice. I am ninety percent positive at least most of these are the right notes. I don't care. It's my song. I own it.

A steady voice rises from the darkness and mingles with mine. It's an echo, I think, but then the voice dips into a pretty harmony that I recognize from dozens of summer nights, and as the chorus rises, it rises too, soaring above me, stronger than me, buoying my song. It's as familiar as his face across the dinner table. Sean. A moment later two or three more voices join in, and then the sound swells around me and I lose count.

Lights constellate here and there, speckling the darkness. Cell phones. People are holding up their cell phones, swaying side to side.

For me.

I can't breathe.

My voice drops out entirely and I stand on the stage and watch as my classmates sing the last chorus without me. It ends on a strange note, one that doesn't sound like an ending, and the voices trail away slowly like they aren't sure we're done here, like maybe there's a coda they forgot.

Then someone yells, "Wild Card!"

And the applause crashes into me and rolls me like the unexpected break of a wave.

Shit.

I'm pretty sure I just rocked that.

9

Mark

"Dude, what the fuck just happened?"

My mom once said that no one had ever told Cody how short he was, and I know what she meant. He's coming at me like a two-hundred-and-fifty-pound defensive tackle. I throw up a hand before he crashes into me and (let's be real) bounces off. "Whoa, calm down."

"Calm down? Fuck, Mark! Your girlfriend is out of control!"

"You're making a scene." The people filing out of the auditorium are stopping, staring at the quarterback getting chewed out by five and a half feet of angry senior class president. I grab his arm and pull him into a corner. "What are you talking about?"

He flings an arm back toward the empty stage. "Did you see that performance? I mean, were you even watching, or were you too busy eyefucking her?"

"I couldn't see her, dumbass, the lights were off."

"Yeah, that's another thing. What the hell happened to the power? I tested everything!"

"It was me, okay? I killed the power."

"Why in fuck's sake—"

"She wants out of the Bowl, I told you."

"Well fucking bad news for her, then. Everyone loved that."

"I don't know why she did that." I run a hand through my hair. "I thought she was doing that song from *The Guardian*."

"The Bodyguard."

"Whatever."

"She *was*. She's not allowed to just change it, that's against the rules."

"Dude, who cares?"

"It's supposed to be the contestants trying to win bids, not create some kumbaya bullshit and make *friends* with everybody."

"What are you, like, mad that she's making friends?"

"She's turning my Prom Bowl into a fucking joke!"

"Okay, calm down."

"We talked about this. You said you had my back."

"I *do* have your back. How come you're not supporting *me*?"

"What the fuck, how am I not supporting you?"

"She's my girlfriend! I want to take her to prom!"

"So fucking *bid*, you're not new!"

"We don't all get Jet Skis for our allowance, asshole."

He stares at me.

"Okay. That was . . . I'm sorry. I didn't mean that."

"What *did* you mean?" he asks.

"I—"

"Hey guys!" Ava pops up out of nowhere. "Holy shit, right?"

"Holy shit," Cody agrees, flatly.

She turns to me. "It was good, right?"

"Ava, could you . . . give us a sec?"

Cody shakes his head. "Don't bother. We're done."

"Cody, man, don't—"

He waves me off. "Forget it, Palmer. I'll see you at practice. If I haven't been cut from the team by then."

Ava watches him walk off. "What's he so upset about?"

"Ava, why did you change your song?"

"You didn't like it?" Her face falls.

"Uh, well, I think everybody *liked* it."

"Whoa. Why are you snapping at me?"

"This isn't a good thing if you want to be eliminated this round, Ava."

She doesn't say anything. She isn't looking at me.

"That's still what you want, right?"

"I mean . . ."

"Ava?"

"I met these girls," she says in a rush. "Some sophomores."

"What sophomores? This happened tonight?"

"At homecoming."

"Okay, so what?"

"So they really liked me. And they're not . . . you know, they didn't think of themselves as the kind of girls who could ever be a part of something like this—"

"Ava, what the hell are you talking about? Jesus!"

"You don't have to yell at me," she says quietly.

I sigh and force myself to calm down. "I don't want to lose you."

"Mark, I think I could actually *win* this thing."

"What?"

"Do you get what that would mean to those girls? To so many girls? Do you have any idea what it's like when an underdog gets a win and you've never had one?"

"This isn't *Remember the Titans*, Ava. You're not breaking down social barriers here. You're just killing our shot at going to our senior prom together because you're getting caught up in the game."

"Getting caught up in it? Mark, I *am* in it. I didn't choose it."

"You're choosing it right now." I feel the tension creeping up my back, like when I'm stuck on the bench watching the defensive line blow a lead.

"Are you seriously mad at me because I did a good job?"

"Don't you even want us to go to prom together?"

"Maybe we still can."

"Yeah. Maybe. Maybe I'll win the lottery tomorrow. Maybe someone will start a rumor about you having VD and no one will bid on you."

She stares. "You don't have to be such a jerk."

Ouch. She's not wrong. I *am* being a jerk. But Ava's the one who's changing the playbook in the middle of the game, staring at me like I'm not worth her time because I don't have the money to pay for her. I don't know what her deal is all of a sudden. But from where I'm standing right now, it looks like my girlfriend is going to be with another guy on prom night—fucking *fuck*.

The letter from Notre Dame is so precisely placed in the center of my desk that I can tell my mom was the one who delivered it. I can see her carefully setting it down, stepping back, then stepping forward to adjust the angle. She's downstairs now, her knife whacking rhythmically against the cutting board on the kitchen counter, and it feels like an invasion of privacy. I wish there was a way I could not read this letter right now. I wish I could walk back downstairs without feeling her eyes trying to pull information from the expression on my face.

I pick up the letter and flop down on my bed.

When a school is interested in me, they don't send a letter. They send a full marketing package. Big, glossy campus brochures, course catalogs, win-loss records, sometimes stickers and T-shirts and stuff like that. I haven't gotten any of these slim envelopes from colleges yet, but I'm familiar with the concept. I know what this is.

God, I am not in the mood for more bad news.

I tear open the envelope and pull out the single piece of paper.

> Dear Mr. Palmer,
>
> Thank you for expressing interest in the Notre Dame football program. Here at NDU we take pride in our exceptional student-athletes. Your

transcript is reflective of a commitment to academics that we admire.

We would love to take a look at your highlight video. This should not exceed five minutes and should represent your best moments on the field throughout your high school career. You may send this via e-mail to josh.kerrington@nduathletics.edu. Please put "Mark Palmer Highlights" in the subject line.

Once again, thank you for reaching out. We look forward to reviewing your video and to determining whether UND is the right fit for you!

With warm regards,

Josh Kerrington
Athletic Director
University of Notre Dame

That's not a no.

It's not a no!

I'm pounding down the stairs like my heels are on fire, tearing into the kitchen and lifting Mom bodily off the ground in a hug.

"Mark!"

"They want to see my video!"

"Mark, put me down!"

I do, and she quickly drops the knife that I did not realize she was still holding on the counter and wipes her hands on her apron. "What's this about a video?"

"Notre Dame! They want to see my video!"

"What video?"

"My playing highlights!"

"Do you have a video of that?"

"I'll cut one together. I have Movie Maker."

"Cut it from what?"

"Game footage. Mom, Notre Dame is interested in me, why are you nitpicking? Aren't you excited?"

"Of course, honey, I just . . ."

"You just what?"

"Well, Mark, all the game footage we have of you are those short video clips Dad takes on his iPad. I don't think those are what the coaches at Notre Dame are looking for."

I can't believe she's being like this. "You *want* me to go to Notre Dame, Mom."

"I know, honey, it's a great school, and it's great that they're interested."

"But what? I should just give up? Because you don't have a high-res camera?"

"I just don't understand where you're going to find footage. That's all."

"I'll talk to Coach."

"Coach Vanguard has only been with you for a few months. How much footage could he have?"

"I'm sure he has some."

"Why don't the Notre Dame recruiters come here to see you? Wouldn't that be easier?"

"Seriously, Mom? Do you want me to ask them? Do you want me to call up Notre Dame athletics and say, hey, I can't put together five minutes of fucking video, would you mind hopping on a plane?"

"Watch your mouth."

"Sorry."

"Maybe you'd better just go back up to your room and calm down."

"Jesus, Mom."

She turns her back to me, picks up her knife, and begins dicing as gently as it is possible to dice a carrot, like nothing is bothering her at all. If it were me I'd bring the blade down hard, take out my frustration on the vegetables. I storm out of the kitchen, feeling like I have to be pissed off for both of us.

Back in my room, I pull out my laptop and go to the Patterson website. The athletic section has recent highlights in both photo and video form. It stopped being thrilling to see myself on screen about a week into freshman year, and I haven't really looked at this since. There are a couple of decent quality clips here, though, and I know Coach Vanguard makes game tapes to review and analyze. I'm sure he's got something I can use.

I pick up my phone and scroll to Cody's name—this is great news, the golden goose, this is Notre Dame and I have to tell someone—but I hesitate at the memory of our fight earlier. I want to believe that Cody would set the bullshit aside and be happy for me right now, but best not to push it. He'll adjust to being second string in a few more weeks, and things will go back to normal. I'll tell him then.

I don't really want to text any of my other teammates, though. Telling them about this before telling Cody would be incredibly awkward. He'd take it as a personal attack.

Really, there's only one other person I want to talk to. And yeah, okay, technically I'm mad at her, but this is so much bigger than Prom Bowl. This is so much bigger than some stupid fight. This is everything I've been dreaming of since I was a little kid.

Before I can talk myself out of it, I'm pulling on my shoes.

10

Ava

Sol and I keep cutting our eyes at each other and making faces at Charlotte when she isn't looking. Normally I would feel bad, except that I've spent the last several weeks listening to Charlotte make stupid judgey comments about other people. So now, when she says Thor is the hottest of the Avengers and Sol rolls her eyes, I have to bite down on my lip to keep from laughing. It's not like Thor being hot is even a particularly hilarious opinion to have. It's just the way she says it, like it's a fact, like she's conferring wisdom upon us. It's so *Charlotte*.

"I think Mark Ruffalo is the hottest," I say.

Charlotte frowns, probably trying to rationalize my disagreement. "That's because you have a boyfriend named Mark."

"What?" I stare at her openly for that one.

"How does that make sense?" Sol asks.

"It's word association," Charlotte says sagely. "Everyone knows about it. It's science. Ava thinks Mark's name is sexy now because he's her boyfriend. All other Marks will forever be sexier to her."

Sol grabs Dad's Sharpie off the coffee table, holds it up, and affects a manly voice. "Ava! It's me, Marker. Quick, help me get my top off!"

I grab the marker away from her and take off its top, and Sol falls right over on the floor in a fit of laughter.

"I thought you two were fighting," Charlotte says. "Marlee said you were getting catty in the greenroom."

"Is that a fact?" For a moment I'm tempted to tell Charlotte what I know about Marlee. "She got her story wrong."

"We're not fighting," Sol agrees with the air of an indignant child. The truth is that the fight dissipated as quickly as it began. Sol was the first one to hug me when I stepped offstage after my song. I apologized, and now it's like nothing happened between us. I don't know whether to chalk it up to performance anxiety or what, but what I do know is that I've never de-escalated tension so quickly with anyone but my brother.

Charlotte, clearly over the conversation, waves her hand to shut us up. I don't really know why we're watching the movie she picked, since Sol suggested *Ratatouille* and I'd much rather have watched that. I'm not even sure why Charlotte is here at all. I called Dad from school after the talent show to ask if Sol could spend the night, and somehow by the time he arrived at school to pick us up it had been arranged that Charlotte was coming over too. Dad and Aunt Claire must be more committed to the idea of us being friends than I'd realized.

Dad comes into the living room now with a big bowl of

his specialty stovetop popcorn and sets it down in front of us. "Ladies."

Charlotte reaches out with a toe and edges the bowl away from her. "I'm maintaining."

Solstice grabs the bowl and pulls it toward her. "Thanks, Mr. Vanguard."

"Call me Coach," he says with a grin. He always does that. It's obnoxious. He isn't Sol's coach.

"Guys," Charlotte complains. On screen, Thor is tossing his long hair and swinging his hammer in slow motion.

The doorbell rings, and a half-second later Sean comes streaking through the living room as if he'd been on starting blocks. My brother loves answering the door, answering the phone, getting the mail, anything that offers the possibility of someone trying to socialize with him.

I hear the door shuck open and a familiar voice asks, "Is Ava here?"

Dad moves toward the hallway. "Is that Mark Palmer?"

This time a look passes between me and Charlotte and it is one hundred percent *oh crap*. Dad doesn't know about me and Mark. I've never had a boyfriend. This isn't how I'd have wanted to break the news to him at all.

Dad reenters the living room looking mildly puzzled. "Ava? You have a guest."

Mark's contrite, head down, twisting his car keys in his hands. "Can we talk, Ava?"

Right. I'm mad at him. Because he's a giant jerk. "I'm kind of busy."

"Just for a minute?"

I'm tempted to tell him to go ahead and talk if he wants to, but Dad and Charlotte and even Sol are watching us like we're the world's most interesting badminton game, and I really don't want this to be a public conversation. "Outside then."

Mark's car is a beat-up Dodge Neon that looks like his mom picked it out for him. We sit on the trunk with our feet on the bumper and don't look at each other.

"I'm sorry," he says, after a beat.

"What are you even sorry for?"

"I don't know. Not supporting you?"

"You know I literally have to compete in this stuff, right?"

"I know."

"You know I tried to get out of it from the start."

"Yeah."

"And I'm trying to throw it. It's not my fault that everything keeps getting messed up."

"I said I was sorry."

"It's like the point of the Wild Card is to suck at everything for entertainment and you're mad that I'm not doing it right."

"It's not like that," he mumbles.

"No, I'm telling you it *is* like that. That's how it feels. You can't tell me I'm wrong about how I feel." Even as I hear myself, I can't believe I'm talking to Mark like this. I guess I'm still riding the adrenaline from the talent show or something. I wonder if this is what it feels like to be drunk.

"Every time you do well in one of these things, I have to deal with the possibility of losing you," he says, rubbing his thumbs together nervously.

"I just keep thinking of those other girls," I say. "I felt like that when I was younger, you know? Like I couldn't measure up to girls like Charlotte and Caity and Sol. Like a guy like you . . . would never want me." My face heats up and I study the grass. I can't look at him.

"I want you," Mark says quietly.

"Yeah, I know."

"I'm sorry I went off on you like that. Cody was being a dick and I took it out on you."

"I could tell."

"So are we okay?"

He's looking at me expectantly, like *of course we're okay*, because how could we not be now that he's apologized. I don't want it to be that easy for him. I want him to work for it. But what am I supposed to say? He's sorry.

"Yeah," I say. "We're good."

He grins and cups my cheek with his hand and for a minute I think he's about to kiss me, but he doesn't. "I have the best news," he says.

"What is it?"

Before he can answer, I hear the screen door bang and I jerk two inches away from Mark reflexively. Dad's coming down the porch steps into the yard, with Sol and Charlotte scampering after him like nervous terriers.

"Ava!" he yells.

"Here, Dad."

I see him spot us and alter his trajectory. He stops in front of us and plants his hands on his hips, and for a minute I think he's about to curse me out for calling a penalty against his team. "Want to tell me what's going on?"

Shit. I glance at Sol. She jerks her head toward Charlotte, who is just eating this up.

I'm about to answer—I know Dad's you're-not-getting-out-of-here-until-I'm-satisfied glare—but it's Mark who speaks up. "Yes sir, sorry." And I remember, suddenly and jarringly, that my boyfriend and my father have a relationship that has nothing to do with me.

"Ava and I have been seeing each other for a few weeks," Mark says. "I came to congratulate her on her performance at the talent show tonight. Everyone's talking about what a good job she did."

"Is that right." Dad doesn't give anything away. I have no idea if I'm in trouble here. Was I supposed to bring Mark home and introduce him when we began dating? Wouldn't that have been redundant, since he and Dad already know each other? I'm not sure. Dad's never told me what the rules are for me and boys. Maybe he never thought I'd have occasion to need any rules.

"Yes sir," Mark says.

"You and my daughter?"

"We have some classes together, and we both . . . like football?" Mark struggles with a question that wasn't asked.

"And you say she performed well tonight?"

"She sang 'We Are the Champions.'"

"Not much of a singer, my Ava."

God. Kill me.

"Stage presence," Sol speaks up. "They say it's nine-tenths of the show."

I wait, chewing on my lip.

Suddenly Dad laughs, big and booming. "Well, hell! Isn't that something, Peanut? Good for you!"

I think I'm going to melt off the car into a pile of humiliated viscera. "Thanks Dad."

Dad claps Mark on the back. "Come on inside and have a soda."

So I guess *that's* going to be a thing.

Charlotte runs after the guys and I hear her receding voice pestering Mark about whether he saw her perform and did he think she was any good. Thank God I accepted his apology quickly instead of putting up a fuss. If he has to put up with my family, the least I can do is be uncomplicated.

Sol takes my hand and helps me down from the trunk. "You okay?"

"What just happened?"

"Charlotte made some tacky-ass joke about you two getting physical out here and your dad overheard. You weren't, right?"

"We were talking. God, that's gross, in front of my dad?"

"Well, it's Charlotte."

"Yeah."

She wraps an arm around me. "Hey, it's probably for the best, you know?"

"No. How?"

"At least you already know your dad likes Mark."

"Why doesn't that make me feel any better?"

"Because you're an Olympic-caliber worrier." She smiles. "Let's go find out what happens to the Avengers."

"Oh God, we'd better get back before Charlotte starts explaining her scientific theories to Mark."

Sol laughs and sets the pace back to the house, tugging me in her wake.

PATTERSON HIGH PROM BOWL

Private

Cody Spencer

Posted 1 min ago

Reminder to Prom Bowl contestants—THIS IS NOT A GAME.

Prom Bowl is a tradition at Patterson that means a lot to a lot of people. It's not an appropriate place to make some kind of point about feminism or anarchy or whatever your pet soapbox issue may be. Your job is to compete to the best of your ability in the events as they have been designed.

Okay, with that said, let's get back to the fun—round two results! A few surprises this round! Remember, the number next to your name is the highest bid you've received. Now is the time for those of you in the top five to alert your boyfriends how much it'll cost to score your company for prom.

For those of you on the bottom half, you ran a great race. Hope you like the guy who got you!

Hannah Bauman—$100
Amy Spicoli—$100
Denise Mellibosky—$160
Maria Baker—$220
Marlee Wheeler—$240

Kylie Richards—$260
Charlotte Ramsey—$260
Caity Pierce—$300
Solstice Downing—$300
Ava Vanguard—$340

Like • Reply

---

0 Comments

MEMBERS
Cody Spencer
Mark Palmer
Caity Pierce
Hannah Bauman
Amy Spicoli
Solstice Downing
Charlotte Ramsey
Denise Mellibosky
Kylie Richards
Marlee Wheeler
Maria Baker
Wild Card: Ava Vanguard

11

Mark

So.

Safe topics:

Football. (State champions! Yeah!)

Schoolwork.

Our families—she's meeting mine for the first time tonight, and everyone's stupid with nerves about it. Ava's been texting me all day, and Mom actually put her hair in curlers.

Also, movies. I showed her the little indie theater that reruns the classics on Saturdays, and we've been going every week. Tomorrow it's Back to the Future, which Ava hasn't seen. Sometimes I have to question Coach Vanguard's parenting, honestly.

Unsafe topics:

Prom Bowl. We haven't discussed it since the talent show. I don't know what her plan is for the final event. All I know is that I don't have the current winning bid on my girlfriend, and I don't have the money it would take to get her. Which means we have to add another unsafe topic to the list. . . .

Prom itself. Last word was that we were going together, but

it doesn't look like that's happening now. So should I make other plans? Ask another girl? How do you ask your girlfriend if you should ask another girl to the prom? But then, she's the one who started taking the competition all seriously, so maybe she should have to answer the question. I don't know.

Not to mention money. Like, what am I supposed to say to her? Sorry, Ava, I really do want to go to prom with you, but you're too expensive? Yeah, that's not emasculating at all.

Our friends. Because my best friend is running the Prom Bowl and her friends are all competing in it.

But as long as we stay away from any of that stuff, everything's fine.

Ava meets me in the hall outside the conference room at the local Sheraton Hotel, where the end-of-season banquet is being held. She's wearing a pretty dress, pale pink with a fitted top and one of those flippy skirts that fan out when a girl spins around. "You look good," I say.

"Thanks." She runs her hands over the dress, brushing away invisible lint. "Excited?"

"Nervous."

"Why? The offer's finalized, right?"

"It's done. I sent them my acceptance."

"So you're gonna be a Fighting Irish?"

"A Fighting Irish*man*, I think."

"I don't think so. They're not the Notre Dame Fighting Irishmen."

"So they're just a massive force of nationality?"

"Yeah, I'm pretty sure. Like how Tulsa is the Golden Hurricane, or Tulane is the Green Wave."

"The *Green Wave*?"

"Anyway, if you're already in, what are you nervous about?"

"I don't know. Cody finding out, I guess."

"Cody doesn't know?"

"Nobody on the team knows."

"*Mark.* Why haven't you told him?"

"Because . . ." I don't know. Because he's been so obnoxious lately. Because he acts like everything I do is somehow targeting and victimizing him, and every bad thing that happens to him is somehow my fault. Because when he finds out I got the Notre Dame bid, he's going to suck all the awesomeness out of it like a Dementor. I just want to be happy about this and not have it ruined.

"I don't know," I tell her.

She squeezes my hand. "You should tell him."

"Ava . . ."

"He'd probably rather hear it from you than from my dad, right?"

"Why are you so nice?"

"I'm really not that nice."

"Yeah, you're like Mother Teresa if Mother Teresa was hot."

"Okay, first of all, that is a very weird thing to say. Are you telling me you can't think of any women who are nice *and* hot?"

"Well, there's you . . ."

"Ha ha. Second of all, Mother Teresa wasn't that nice. The woman ran some seriously sketchy hospitals."

"You're smart too." I tug her close.

"You know your parents are, like, ten feet away, right?"

"Mmm, they'll survive."

"Yeah, this isn't really the first impression I was hoping to make." She's not pulling away though.

"Want to go find an empty room?"

"You need to go find Cody."

"You do not even like Cody."

"*You* like Cody. And I like you."

"See? Nice." I kiss her. We've gotten better at it. I guess all those nights in the back of the theater weren't for nothing. I wonder if Ava has turned into an all-around good kisser now, or if she's just perfect for me. I wonder this in the part of my brain that isn't on fire with the knowledge that she's pressed up against me. It's a very small section of brain. Ava is taking up most of me.

She detaches. "Go find Cody. I'll go say hi to your parents."

"Are you okay to do that?" The girl I met three months ago would have been too shy to walk up to someone's parents and introduce herself.

"I'm good," she says.

I find Cody, finally, by following the squish-crack sounds of a fist meeting a face.

It's really fucked up that I associate that sound with my best friend.

He's in the alley behind the Sheraton, between a couple of Dumpsters, shirt untucked and dirty, tie pulled loose, and he's holding someone against the wall with his whole forearm. I move to see who it is, but my view is blocked as Cody winds up for another swing.

"Hey!"

Cody drops his fist in surprise and loses his grip on the kid, who slips out of his grasp and runs down the alley away from us. Away from me. Because for all that kid knows, I'm out here to help Cody beat him up. I catch Cody by the collar before he can give chase. "What the hell?"

"He gave me lip." Cody tries to jerk out of my grip, but fails.

"You're bleeding, man."

He looks down at his hand. "That isn't mine."

"Cody . . . Jesus."

"What?"

"You're going to get suspended, you know. Or worse. You can't just—"

"They did it to us, didn't they?"

"*They* didn't do *shit* to us. That kid never did anything to you."

"It's tradition."

"Oh, what are you, the Fiddler on the Roof?"

"The fiddler was an allegory, dumbass."

"You can't just beat the crap out of people for *no reason at all* and then say it's because you got pushed around as a freshman. That's not tradition, that's just you being bitter and actually kind of pathetic."

"Are you calling me a bully?" he demands.

"No, I'm not saying that, okay?"

"What *are* you saying?"

"I'm just saying . . . go easy on the freshmen."

He shakes his head. "You put a hell of a spin on it, Palmer."

"What does that mean?"

"Every time you talk about freshman year, it's like you think I spent the whole time getting punched on."

"Well . . ." Come on, man, don't make me say it.

"Those guys gave me hell, yeah, but after the season was over we were tight. Sophomore year, who do you think set me up with Laura Baretta? Who do you think got me my fake ID?"

"Because you let them beat you up?"

"Because I didn't run squealing like a pig every time something happened, so they knew they could trust me."

"You're saying I didn't get beat up freshman year because nobody trusted me?"

"You never wanted a fake ID, Mark. You never wanted to smoke weed at Roseman's house. Besides, you were already tapped to be first string Varsity quarterback in a few years, so it's not like you had to play the game. You've never had to."

"That isn't true."

"Whatever, man. We should get inside."

I grab his arm to stop him. "Cody."

"Get off."

"Just hang on—"

"You don't want to keep Notre Dame waiting." He shakes free of me and walks off.

Fuck.

How did he find out?

How long has he known?

We always said we'd go to college together. When we were little, running around his backyard and pitching to each other with a Nerf basketball because we didn't own a football, the plan was peewee league, high school, college, and then the pros. The teams changed depending on our mood and who was doing well that year, but the plan was a constant. I've known for a while now that Cody isn't up to Division I standards—and I don't think he would disagree—but I guess I thought he would still be happy for me.

I'd be happy for him. I mean, I'm not going to try to pretend I don't have the better deal here, but if the situation were reversed I'd be congratulating him.

Maybe this is good though. Maybe now that everything's out in the open, we'll be fine. Of course we'll be fine. It's me and Cody. He's always been kind of a hothead, and I don't blame him for being upset that he had to hear it from someone else, but it'll blow over. As soon as I get the chance, I'll take him out for burritos and we'll talk about it.

I go back inside and take my seat in the horseshoe of Patterson football players.

Across from me, among the JV kids, I see Sean Vanguard, my girlfriend's little brother, wipe a trickle of blood from his nose.

Fuck.

PATTERSON HIGH PROM BOWL

Private

Cody Spencer

Posted 1 min ago

Girls Gone Wild Party
December 12, 9 pm—2 am
3782 Cherry Blossom Court, Duluth, MN 55802

SHHH! It's time for the annual Girls Gone Wild party, the final event of the Prom Bowl and official kickoff to the holiday season! As your class president, I have the honor of hosting.

Rules:
DO make arrangements with your parents to be out all night. If you bail on the party and can't compete, that is your problem.
DON'T tell your parents where you will actually be.
DO believe the hype—this is the best party of the year.
DON'T call last year's seniors and ask what to expect.
That's patently forbidden, and they will turn you in if you try it.
DO come prepared to cut loose.
DON'T pregame (trust me).

Bonus points if: you bring a bottle of something
Seniors only, RSVP, and keep it on the DL!

---

89 going • 30 maybe • 214 invited

Caity Pierce

Looking forward to it :)

Posted 5 sec ago • **Like** • **Reply**

MEMBERS

Cody Spencer
Mark Palmer
Caity Pierce
Solstice Downing
Charlotte Ramsey
Kylie Richards
Wild Card: Ava Vanguard

12

Mark

"I can't believe the school is fine with this," Ava grumbles as we walk up the driveway to Cody's front door.

"It's not a school-sponsored thing," I say.

"Okay, but Prom Bowl is, like, the most widely publicized event at Patterson. Teachers have actually pressured me about it. My dad even knows about it."

"Does your dad know where you are tonight?"

"He thinks I'm at Charlotte's."

"Exactly."

"None of the staff knows about this party?"

"It's kind of a don't ask, don't tell situation," I say. "Everyone knows the bids go up one more time after the second event, but none of the teachers ever ask about it."

"I can't *believe* the school is fine with this."

Murph Williams answers the door wearing an orange mesh vest from gym class over his T-shirt. He holds out a plastic mixing bowl. "Cell phones."

Ava's hand goes to her pocket. "What?"

"Hand over your phones."

I pull mine out of my pocket, make sure the security lock is on, and drop it into the bowl. It clacks against the pile of phones Murph's already collected. "It's fine, Ava."

"Why do we have to hand over our phones?" she asks, suspicion clouding her voice.

"Because you won't be let into the party otherwise." Murph leers, and I kind of want to slap him.

Ava tugs at my arm. "Maybe we should just go, Mark."

"Ava?"

"Sean?"

He's coming down the stairs with a bathroom-size trash can in his hands, also wearing an orange vest. "What are you doing here? I thought you were going to stay at Aunt Claire's."

"I'm in the Prom Bowl, idiot."

His eyes widen. "You're one of the girls that's going to go wild?"

"What did you think?"

"I didn't know this was a Prom Bowl thing. Cody just said it was a senior party."

"And you didn't think there was any way I might be at one of those?"

"Well . . ." He grimaces and I can tell that's exactly what he thought.

Ava tosses her phone at him, underhand, and he moves the garbage can to catch it. "Don't drink or I'll tell Dad," she warns.

"Yeah, yeah." Sean waves her off.

I pluck at Ava's sleeve as she leads the way into the house. "Your brother's friends with Cody?"

"Apparently."

"I kind of thought they didn't get along."

"Sean gets along with everybody."

Seriously? She hasn't noticed him coming home scraped up, with bloody noses? Or is he explaining that away somehow? In which case, was Cody right the night of the awards banquet, and everyone but me understands that the seniors are beating on the underclassmen as part of some weird trust-building exercise?

And does the fact that Sean's here tonight mean he passed the test?

Cody and I always went to parties together. Now I'm trying to remember if anyone ever came up to me and singled me out for an invitation. Even tonight, I'm only here because the entire senior class was invited. How much of my high school social status has been bullshit, predicated on the fact that I'm the quarterback, or that I'm Cody's friend? Cody's always been the one calling me up and letting me know where the action is. Without him, would I just be some student athlete loner?

I find Cody in the kitchen, pulling a baking sheet of Jell-O shots out of the fridge. "Mark! Hey!"

It's awkward. We haven't really spoken since the banquet, and now here he is acting like everything's normal. "Hi."

"Brought your girl, I see."

Ava falls back a pace.

"Are . . . we cool?" I ask.

"Dude." Cody jumps up to sit on the granite countertop, which puts him approximately at my eye level, and grabs both my shoulders. "We are so cool. We are the coolest of cukes."

"Cukes?"

"Cucumbers," Ava surmises.

"You're here, and I'm here, and the girls are going to get wild and it is *senior year*, man, enough drama, right? Enough *bullshit*."

"Hey, no argument here." He's drunk, but that doesn't mean that he's wrong.

He points at Ava. "You need to get your cute butt into the living room. The games are about to begin."

She looks at me, and for the first time since the fashion show, I think maybe she needs saving.

"Go on," I tell her. "I'll be right behind you."

She lingers for a second, waiting for I don't know what, and then turns and walks into the living room.

"You know, I'm starting to see it," Cody says. "She's pretty hot. In, like, a soap commercial way."

"What?"

"You know those commercials with the fat naked girls who use soap and love their bodies?"

"You're drunk."

"It's a *party*." He pushes an empty cup into my hand. "The action's in the living room."

I wait for him to leave and then go to the countertop where the bottles of liquor and mixers are set out. I fill my cup with Coke. Freshman year, the night of my first game and first post-game party, my dad grabbed me in the parking lot and told me to carry around a cup of soda. "No one will bother you about drinking if they think you already have something," he said. I mean, I still drink at parties sometimes, sure, but it seems like a lot of people don't realize it's optional.

"Everybody in the living room!" Cody calls. "We're getting started!"

Cody's living room is standing room only. The sectional couch and coffee table have been pushed up against the walls to make more space, but I still can't get more than a couple of steps into the room. I don't see Ava anywhere.

Cody climbs up onto the couch and waves his arms over his head. "Everyone quiet down, okay? Let's get the rules out there."

Someone boos him. Someone else tries to start up a chant of "Girls go wild! Girls go wild!" It doesn't really get off the ground, but it does send fresh adrenaline through the crowd. The room feels charged and dangerous and I don't like it. Suddenly I'm wishing I'd grabbed Ava and gotten out of here when I had the chance.

Then the crowd parts a little and I see her.

She's standing in a line with the other four girls, looking desperately out of place, hugging herself and scanning the crowd. I try to push forward a little in case she's looking for me. Some guy I don't know scowls and nudges me back.

"The point of tonight's event," Cody says, "is to give the ladies a chance to show us who would be the most fun after prom."

The way he says "fun" doesn't sound like anything fun.

Cody signals with his hand like an emcee and Murph and Sean appear with a keg on a hand truck. They settle it on the floor in front of the line of girls. Sean looks anxious as hell, his gaze darting around like a bird and landing on everything but Ava. He looks like I feel.

"It's a beer chugging contest!" Cody yells, and a cheer goes up. "One for one until you puke or pass out."

Ava's cousin Charlotte bounces up and down on her toes like she's eager for the opportunity to drink herself into a damn coma for our entertainment. Like that's not something she could do any night of the week. This cannot be what happens every year. Is this really the best Cody could come up with? He doesn't really think these girls are going to *do* it, does he?

Fuck, these girls aren't really going to do it, are they?

Sean taps the keg and I watch confusion, shock, and sadness chase each other across Ava's face.

Ava

Since when does Sean know how to tap a keg? I don't even know how to tap a keg. Does Sean drink?

Charlotte gulps down her first beer like a pro and hands her cup back to Cody. He draws a tally mark on the side of it and hands it back to Sean for a refill. On Charlotte's other side, I can see Kylie, the dancer, finishing her first drink too.

I turn to Solstice. "This is crazy."

She takes a cup from Cody and drinks the whole thing in one long swallow. "What is?"

"Are you seriously going along with this?"

"You're up, Wild Card." Cody holds out a beer to me.

I hold up my hands. "No, I pass."

"You can't pass," someone yells from the crowd.

"Did she *pass*?"

"Can she do that?"

"She can't do that."

"Can he make her do it?"

"She's the Wild Card. How else does she expect to get a date?"

"She has to do it."

"Wild Card! Wild Card!"

They're pressing closer. The floor space around me is disappearing, and I'm not going to be able to break through this crowd. My head spins. I have to get out of here. Where the hell is Mark? I catch Sean's eye instead. *Help.*

"Everyone calm down," Cody's speaking in that sportscaster voice again, the event coordinator of my humiliation. "Nobody has to drink if they don't want to."

The responding *booooo* tightens my throat.

"Guys! We can't make anyone drink. That's, like, illegal. The decent thing is to give these girls choices, right? I mean, there are more ways to be fun after prom than just getting drunk." Cody grins like the big bad wolf.

"Take your shirt off!" someone hollers.

"Take something off," Cody agrees, "or you can kiss one of the other ladies."

Catcalls. My classmates have become one entity, blurring and yelling, and for some reason the only face I can pick out is Sean's. He's standing by the keg, one of the plastic cups in hand, staring at me. Waiting to see what I'll do.

I have to keep this under control. I have to stay in charge of this situation. I won't be able to do that if I'm drunk off my ass.

On my right, I see Caity grab Solstice for a kiss. Solstice goes with it for a minute, but then she pushes Caity off and holds her cup out to Murph for a refill. I think I might throw up.

"Everybody hold up!" Cody yells. "Pause! Fucking *pause*!"

He's going to call it off. He knows this is getting out of hand. He's going to end the contest here and just let people bid. He has to.

He fixes his eyes on me. "Ava?"

I look for a gap in the crowd. There isn't one.

I swallow. "Okay."

"A drink?"

"No, I'll take something off." I keep my eyes on Cody. I don't want to look at Sean. No one would stop *him* from leaving, right? I'm sure he doesn't want to watch me do this any more than I want to do it.

"Ava! Ava!" Cody waves his hand like a conductor, and some others join in. There's nothing supportive about this chant. They didn't even use my name when they chanted for me after the talent show and it still felt better than this. This is a dare. This is a threat.

I reach up and pull the elastic from my hair.

Cody falls silent. The chant continues around him.

I flick the elastic at him like a rubber band. "One point."

"More!"

"Keep going!"

I scan the crowd for Mark. I don't see him. He wouldn't have left, right? Maybe he's still in the kitchen, picking out something to drink. He'd say something if he knew what was happening.

I kick off my shoes.

Beside me, Solstice slams down another cup of beer. I turn and find Caity on my other side, locking lips with Charlotte, whose legs are now bare under her long sweater. This is moving fast.

"Six points to Caity!" Cody yells. "Four points Charlotte. Four points Kylie. Two points Ava."

"I have three!"

"The shoes count as one. Lose your socks."

I yank them off quickly. If I fall too far behind, everyone will turn their attention back to me. I don't need to win this, but I need to blend in.

"Three points Ava," Cody amends. "Solstice—seven!"

"What?" I grab her arm. "Solstice. Slow down."

"Keep up!" She laughs.

I watch Charlotte drink another beer and then step across Caity to make out with Kylie. Kylie slips her hands under Charlotte's top. A minute later she's holding a bra and Charlotte's hugging herself and giggling.

"Three more for Charlotte! Kylie, take a bonus point for that smooth move."

Caity raises her eyebrows at me suggestively, offering, but I shake my head. I don't want to kiss anyone; I have a boyfriend and he is the only person I've ever kissed and I barely know this girl and I'm not going to do this with everyone staring at me, with *Sean* staring at me. . . .

I unzip my hoodie and drop it to the ground.

"That's four!" Cody yells. "Falling behind, there, Wild Card!"

God, where is Mark? *Help me.*

I unbutton my top.

Slowly.

I'm not sure whether I'm actually going to take it off. I'm still deciding. Maybe I'll just unbutton it and leave it on and hope for a bonus point, like Kylie got.

Or maybe I'll just button it back up and punch people in the face until they get out of my way and I'll run home and fuck all of this.

Something *yanks* me backward and I almost topple onto the floor. I spin around. A boy I don't know is holding my shirt, leaving me naked except for my bra, skirt, and underwear. I bend to grab my hoodie, to cover up, but Cody gets to it first and spins it over his head like a lasso. I hug my bare torso, chilled and humiliated.

"Ten points Solstice!"

What?

She thrusts her arms in the air like a prizefighter, one hand still clutching her beer cup, her eyes unfocused.

"Eleven points Kylie!"

Kylie's in nothing but her panties, pressed up against Caity Pierce, rounding what I'm reasonably sure from my reading is considered second base. How far can this go? At what point do we stop and declare a winner? Or are we waiting until someone passes out or starts having sex right here in the middle of Cody's living room?

"Five points to the Wild Card!"

"Take off your bra!"

"Take off your skirt!"

I'm shaking my head. I'm shaking all over. I'm done. I'm done I'm done I'm done I quit I lose. I turn to find the boy who took my shirt, to get it back so I can get dressed. . . .

Someone grabs me from behind. "Get her bra!"

"No!"

But there are hands, there are hands fumbling at the clasp on my back, and my arms are restrained and I can't fight back and I can't cover up and there's a familiar and horrifying loosening around my ribs and—

“The *fuck*!” someone shouts into my ear.

My arms are released.

My hands fly to my chest, catching, covering, and suddenly he’s there, a big warm wall of Mark. He pulls me against him and all I can feel is how hard I’m shaking, how close I am to tears. I push my face into his soft shirt and breathe, trying to calm down. His hand is so firm on my back that it feels like I’m being held upright. Maybe I am. I let his voice wash over me. He sounds angry, but he isn’t angry at me. I know that. He isn’t talking to me.

“I want to go home.” My lips form the words, but I don’t hear anything. “I want to go home, I want to go home.” I don’t think I’m speaking out loud.

Something warm settles on my shoulders. Someone’s arm.

“Ava.” That’s Mark. “Get dressed, okay? I gotcha.”

I reach around and find the clasp for my bra. I have to slide my fingers under his hand to hook it, and he gives them a little squeeze. *It’s okay.*

“Look out!” Someone yells.

I turn inside the circle of Mark’s arm just in time to see Solstice pitch forward. Her head impacts with the side of the keg and she crumples to the ground, mouth open, eyes closed.

The room goes dead quiet.

13

Ava

"She had ten points, right?" I'm babbling. My hands are all over Solstice, feeling for a pulse or a lump on her head. I'm trying to remember CPR, and whether you're supposed to do it in a case like this. I think I'm supposed to put her in the recovery position. Or is that for something else? Should we not have moved her? No, that's spinal injuries. "Ten points is ten beers. She had *ten beers*?"

"I couldn't see her the whole time," Mark says. "Couldn't some of the points have been for something else?"

"Maybe . . . did she kiss Caity?"

"Wouldn't surprise me."

"Mark!"

Cody pokes his head around the bathroom door. "Is she okay?"

"She needs an ambulance, I think. She's breathing really weird. . . ."

Mark turns to Cody. "Where are the phones?"

"Hang on—"

"We don't have time to hang on!" I shout.

"Mark, get your girl under control!"

Solstice groans a little. That has to be a good sign, right? Comatose people don't groan.

"We can't call anyone," Cody says.

"What?" I can hear the screech in my voice and, God, my mom used to sound like this when she was yelling at my dad. I'm shaking. I'm freezing. My hoodie's gone.

Fuck. Where's Sean?

"We call someone, they'll bust the party."

"The party's *over*, asshole!" I've never heard Mark sound like this. I'm almost scared of him. "She's probably got alcohol poisoning. She needs to get to a hospital."

"So take her. Your girlfriend's out of the running anyway. She hasn't had a drink, she can drive you."

"It's an *emergency*, Cody."

Why are they wasting time arguing? I get to my feet and push past Cody, into the waiting thicket of all my thorny classmates. I can feel their collective stare on my skin like oil and I kind of want to throw up.

"Ava!"

I turn and see the one face I've been looking for all night. "Sean."

He pulls his T-shirt off and hands it to me. "Put this on."

I do. It's tight, too small in the chest and the stomach, but I don't care. "I need my phone. Do you still have them?"

"Over here." He picks his way through the crowd. I grab his sleeve so we won't lose each other. "Is that girl okay?"

"We need to call an ambulance."

"Oh shit."

"You didn't drink, did you?"

"We're not allowed. The freshmen have to do breathalyzers at the end of the party."

"Cody has a breathalyzer?"

"I guess."

"Figures."

Sean hands me the trash can full of nearly identical smartphones. I pour them out on the couch and start pawing through, scanning for my sun-and-star-themed case. Within seconds, hands start reaching into the pile, claiming their phones.

"This one's mine." It's Mark. "Should I call?"

"Should you call? Of fucking course you should call, Mark!"

He stares at me like he doesn't know me. "Okay. Chill."

"Chill?"

"I'm on your side here. You don't have to yell at me."

"Call the fucking ambulance!"

He dials.

"You should get out of here," I tell my brother.

"So should you."

"I will. I have to make sure Charlotte gets out first."

"You can't do that alone."

"Mark's got us. Just go, okay Sean? Go home. I'll be there in an hour."

"Come by my room."

"I will. *Go.*"

He slips off into the crowd.

"Mark?" I grab his arm. "Who's with Solstice?"

"Alcohol poisoning," Mark is saying into the phone. He tips the mouthpiece away and turns to me. "What?"

"Solstice. Who's with her?"

"Uh-huh. 3782 Cherry Blossom Court."

"Who's he on the phone with?" someone asks.

"Did he just give the address?"

"Is he calling the cops?"

The word "cops" is a viral alarm. It spreads from one person to another until I'm hearing it repeated all around me. "The cops are on their way!" "Ditch! The cops are coming!" The room begins to clear. People are shoving at one another, pushing their way to the door. I see a girl fall and my heart is in my goddamn throat until she gets to her feet again. I see Charlotte, eyes half-lidded and skirt half rucked up over her hips, slumped in a chair with my hoodie draped over her like a blanket.

I see my phone.

I don't know why my first instinct in this situation is to document the living hell out of it, but as soon as I've got the phone in my hand I'm taking pictures. I feel like I'm going to need proof that this happened, that this actually was a demented horror show of a night and I didn't make it up or blow it out of proportion. This isn't just me being hysterical or antisocial or the loser Wild Card who doesn't know how to play the game. This is *fucked up.*

"The ambulance is coming," Mark says. "We should bail."

"Who's with Solstice?" I ask again.

"She's fine. The EMTs will be here any minute." He's looking around anxiously, like he thinks they're going to apparate in here Harry Potter–style. "They'll take care of her."

"She's not waiting by herself, are you insane?"

"Ava, we have to get out of here *now*. I'm serious."

"Help me get Charlotte, at least."

"Ava!"

"I'm not leaving her, Mark!"

"Who the fuck called the cops!"

Mark turns. I look past him and see Cody staggering out of the bathroom. He's wild-eyed, scary looking. I can't help it—I step back and put Mark between us.

"Nobody called the cops," Mark says. "We called an ambulance. Solstice needs an ambulance."

"What that bitch needs is to learn to fucking hold her liquor."

"Are you serious?" I sputter. "You're the one who was pushing the beer on us!"

"Haven't you heard of 'Just Say No?'"

"I *did* say no! You told me I had to take my clothes off! You and your friends nearly *assaulted* me!" I can't believe these words are coming out of my mouth. I can't believe I'm actually standing up to him. People are staring. Mark is staring. Oh God.

"Palmer," Cody says, "I'm telling you for the last time, man, get a leash on your dog."

"Fucking *excuse me*?" I step into his space, the way I've seen opposing football players do after a scrimmage, offensive and aggressive as hell.

Cody steps right up to me and hisses, "Underdog. Ugly mutt. Fucking *bitch*."

It feels like everyone in the room draws breath at the same time, a collective gasp that takes up all the oxygen and leaves me short of air. I shouldn't care. I shouldn't care that he put me in the Prom Bowl because he thinks I'm ugly. I shouldn't care that underclassmen see me as a role model because I'm proof that an ugly girl can do it too. I shouldn't care that my own dad and brother know I'm involved in something like this.

I shouldn't care, but I do.

"You're a joke," Cody says, his face twitching as his voice drops to a growl. "You shouldn't even be here. You'd have been out in round one if you weren't fucking Palmer. Slut."

My stomach turns over. I hope to God Sean left when I told him to.

I'm not expecting it when Cody reaches out and grabs me, pulling me against his torso. I try to get free, but he wrenches my arm behind my back. I turn toward him, following the twist of my arm because I'm scared he's going to break or dislocate something and this hurts, fuck, this *really* hurts. . . .

When Sean and I were kids we'd play wrestle and if one of us was too rough we'd call, "Time out." "Time out" meant stop, no questions, hands off, let go. *Let go.* But I can't find the words. I try to kick backward. I hit nothing. I feel Cody's fingers under Sean's T-shirt, moving up my back.

Suddenly, with a sickening wet crunch followed by a thud, the hands on me are gone.

I turn and see Cody on the ground, a hand cupped over his nose and mouth.

Mark is standing above his friend, staring at his fisted hand like it's a stranger.

Fuck.

14

Mark

Cody draws his hand away from his face like he already knows he's going to see blood, like none of this is any surprise to him, and that's unfathomable because there is no possible universe in which I thought I would ever punch Cody Spencer in the face. Cody, who taught me to ride a bike with no hands and carried me home on his handlebars when I wiped out. We get each other's blood on our hands all the time, but not like this. *God.*

This is a mess. This whole thing's a mess. Our prom is going to be an empire built on blood and crazy, and who wants to be the king of that? Let them cancel it. Right now, I don't give a damn. I just want to get out of here, get the blood off my hand, get away from Ava wailing like a siren behind me.

No. No, that's actually a siren.

Shit.

Ava flinches and hiccups when I grab her arm. "Ava, we have to get out of here."

"Solstice . . ."

"The cops are coming. They'll get her, you hear me? We need to bail or we are going to be *arrested*."

She glances back at the bathroom, and for a minute I'm afraid she's going to insist on waiting for the cops to get here. And I know, I *know* that it's so fucked up that a girl is out cold and probably concussed on a bathroom floor and all I can think about is running away. But the thing is, they don't give football scholarships to kids with criminal records, and I can't sacrifice my entire future here. I don't deserve that, do I? I play Varsity. I'm on the student frigging council. I haven't even been drinking tonight.

But my hand and my best friend's face are covered in blood.

Ava finally turns away from the bathroom, thank God. "We have to bring Charlotte."

"Fine." I pull Charlotte upright from the couch. "Can you walk?"

"Mark!" Cody calls from behind us.

Charlotte staggers. "Uh-huh."

Right. I loop an arm around her waist and she slumps against me. "Back door. Through the kitchen," I tell Ava.

"Hey! Don't run away, asshole! This shit is on you too!" Cody's screaming at me like he used to when we were kids and he had temper tantrums. I haven't heard him sound like this in years. "Palmer! Get the fuck back here!"

I don't turn back.

Ava leads the way. The house is mostly empty now, except for the few screw-ups who are too drunk or high to respond to the urgency of the situation. She pushes through the swinging door into the kitchen and holds it for me, and I blink as my eyes try to adjust to a fully lit room. A bottle of something green is tipped over on the counter and running onto the floor, and it looks like someone's ditched out halfway through mopping it up with cocktail napkins. The back door's standing open; clearly we're not the only ones to have this idea.

"To the car?" Ava asks, veering left as we step into Cody's tiny, fenced-in yard.

"We'll never make it. We'd have to go right by the cops."

"Then where . . . ?"

"Come on." Thank God for Cody's parents never fixing the hole in the fence. When we were kids, it was our secret passageway through Hogwarts or our escape route from velociraptors. I crawl through and then Ava pushes Charlotte after me so I can drag her along by her wrists.

"My outfit," Charlotte groans. "Ruined."

"You better hope that's all that's ruined," I snap.

Ava comes through last, waving away my offer of help, and dusts off her knees. "We need to get her home, Mark."

"Do you know where she lives?"

She nods. "It's nearby, I'm pretty sure. Sawmill Road?"

"I know where it is."

Charlotte doubles over and vomits all over her strappy sandals.

Fantastic.

I know this neighborhood as well as my own. Sawmill Road runs parallel to Cody's street, one block over. Charlotte's house is the one with the trout mailbox, which I always loved growing up. I'm mostly carrying her by the time we get there, but I shake her a little and she sees where we are and snaps out of it.

"Her parents are home, right?" I ask Ava, watching Charlotte wobble her way up the walk to the front door.

"Yeah. Don't worry."

"Come on. We should get moving."

"What?"

"If they see her come in like that, they're going to look outside to see who she was with."

Ava shakes me off. "They already know she was with me. Seriously? That's what you're worried about?"

"I . . ." I don't know what I'm worried about. Everything. I cradle my hand and feel the sting of my split knuckles. I just want the last few hours to go away, to evaporate. I don't want Charlotte's parents to see me, because I don't want any witnesses. Because the truth of the matter is maybe there were mitigating circumstances, but I resorted to violence tonight. At the end of the day, how is that really different from Cody bullying freshmen in the locker room? How am I any better than he is?

Maybe the only reason this blood is on my hand and his face, instead of the other way around, is that I'm bigger.

Charlotte makes it to her front door and inside. Ava turns and starts walking without a word, forcing me to chase after her. It's a little farther to her house, about six blocks, but they're all pretty safe and quiet streets. Still, I'm not about to let her walk home by herself.

I catch up with her, but she speeds up again, pulls ahead.

"Ava?"

No answer.

"Are you pissed at me?"

"What do you think?"

"I know things got out of hand back there—"

She barks a laugh. "And where were you, Mark? When things were getting *out of hand*?"

"I couldn't get through that crowd. Nobody could."

"This is why I didn't want to be part of your stupid Prom Bowl in the first place."

"It's not *my* Prom Bowl."

"I asked you to take me off the list."

"And I told you, I couldn't."

"You told me you *wouldn't*. Because it's *so important* to have your stable of compliant girls to bid on, right? The whole senior class would be heartbroken if one person wanted to opt out and you just *couldn't do that to them*. But you didn't give a damn about what you were doing to me."

"What I was doing to you? I've been trying to help you! I've been doing everything I can think of to get you out of this, and *you* keep screwing it up!"

She stops walking so abruptly that I have to swerve to keep from colliding with her. "What?"

Shit.

She looks up at me, narrowed eyes, lips furiously tight, and

I can see she's putting the pieces together. "The slushy," she says.

Her voice is loud and resonant in the night air. I want to melt into the pavement.

"And the talent show? The power failure?"

I don't know what to say. I make an in-depth study of my shoes.

"It was you."

"Ava—"

"You've been *sabotaging* me."

"You didn't want to win!"

"I didn't want to *compete*. If this was about what I wanted, you'd have helped me get my name off the list when I asked you to."

She's got me there.

"So what, is it part of the game? Trolling the Wild Card? You're trying to make me even more of a joke contestant?"

"No! I—I wanted to take you to prom, all right?"

She stares at me. "What?"

"I wanted to bid on you as my prom date, but I knew I wouldn't be able to afford to buy you in the final round."

"You wanted me to be *cheap* so you could *afford* me?" Her features scrunch into the same expression Coach Vanguard wears when I blow an easy play. Disgust. Disappointment. "You could have just gotten me out of the Bowl and asked me to prom like a normal human. In fact, you *did* ask me to prom. What, does it not count unless you pay my fee? What the fuck do you think I am?"

"I told you, I couldn't let everyone down. The fundraiser—"

"Oh my God, shut up about the fucking fundraiser. You're as creepy and misogynistic as everyone else at this fucking school, Mark. You've got no problem buying a girl for the night as long as she's in your budget. It's sick, you know that? You're sick."

"And you're a hypocrite."

"Excuse me?"

"All that bullshit about wanting to use your platform to set an example? What example, that you're a good singer? That you're too good to drink a beer but you're not above taking your clothes off?"

Her eyes widen. She looks slapped, but my head is buzzing and my jaw is grinding and my fists are clenching and I can't stop. She's so self-righteous. She thinks she's so much better than all of us, so much better than a tradition that's been going on since before we were born. She's not any better than me.

"You were just afraid no one would bid on you," I tell her. "You were afraid you'd go out first because you're the Wild Card, and because you're . . ."

"Because I'm *what*?"

"I don't know."

"Because I'm not one of the hot chicks?"

"I didn't say that."

"You didn't have to."

"All the other girls just went along with it. If you wanted the attention, you didn't have to act all noble to get it."

"I don't want *any* of this!"

"Bullshit. You like it. You like people thinking you're cute and fun and one of the most interesting girls in school. There's nothing wrong with that. Just *admit* it."

"Oh, fuck you, Mark."

"Answer the question."

"You didn't ask a question! You just said what you thought and assumed it was right like you always do, Quarterback Mark."

No. I don't do that. "Ava . . . I'm just trying to *help* you."

"Leave me alone." She turns and stalks away up the block, the clicks of her high heels scolding me as she goes.

I know I should follow her, but I don't.

15

Ava

I read about an artist once who did his best work after intense trauma. He'd go into a fugue state, totally dissociating from his identity and everything that made him who he was, and get lost in painting for hours. I don't know how much truth there was to it, but I remember thinking at the time that if you had to put yourself through something horrible like that to make art, maybe you just weren't meant to be an artist.

I don't know why I keep thinking about this.

I haven't touched my homework all day. It's strange. I have a Chem lab due for fifteen percent of my grade, I know how important it is, but I don't care.

Sean knows something's up. We haven't spoken since the party, and I haven't come out of my room, either. I've noticed him sneaking past my door, footsteps slowing to linger for a minute longer than is necessary. I don't know what he's waiting for. A lecture? An explanation? Don't bother, Sean. I'm not your mom. I'm just your fuck-up sister.

The clock on my laptop clicks over to 10:10, the magic time

I made myself hold out for before checking my phone. I haven't looked at it yet this morning. The fact that I waited, that I made it, means there will be a message from Solstice. Or about Solstice. There has to be.

I check.

No missed calls.

No texts.

Nothing from Solstice.

Nothing from Mark.

Not that I even want to hear from him, because apparently he's sold on ideas about me that are such bullshit it's like he doesn't know me at all. I'm not in this for the *attention*. I mean, I want to set an example, but that's not the same as showing off. Right?

I play a couple of rounds of Temple Run on my phone, then open a yoga app I downloaded once and flip through the workouts I've never tried. I'm not going to look at the pictures. I'm not going to look at the pictures. I'm just not.

Oh, who am I kidding.

I click into my photo library.

Cody's house looks like a crime scene. Dim lighting, garbage everywhere, weird focal points like a foot or an arm. Maybe it *is* a crime scene. I still don't know what happened to Solstice. When a girl drinks so much beer she falls down and gets concussed, or worse, is that a crime? Does underage drinking count as a crime if you don't get caught? Does holding my arms and unhooking my bra count?

I need to stop staring at my phone. I'll check again at 10:30, and until then . . . I don't know. I should try to eat something. I haven't eaten since before the party last night.

There's a tap at the door. "Ava?"

"Come in."

Dad pokes his head in. "Got a minute?"

"Okay."

He sits on the bed and slaps his knees like he's bracing for a pep talk. "I just got a call from Aunt Claire."

"Oh?" My stomach turns to Jell-O.

"Apparently Charlotte came home drunk last night."

I'm probably going to be sick.

"I don't imagine I'm telling you anything you don't know," he says. "Since you two were out together."

"Dad—"

"So, where were you ladies, really?"

There's no way I can get out of it. And honestly, it's a relief. I need someone to know about what happened. Dad to the rescue. "We were at a party."

"Was it fun?"

"It—what?"

"Did you have a good time?"

It's so categorically the wrong question to ask that for a moment I can't figure out how to answer it. "Not really."

"Whose party? A friend of Charlotte's?"

"Yeah. Kind of."

"Well, good for you."

"Seriously?"

"I wish you hadn't lied to me. That's unacceptable. But I'm happy you decided to get out and make some new friends, Bear."

He hasn't called me Bear since I was ten. "Thanks, Dad."

"I'm proud of you, Ava. You made good choices, and you got your cousin home safe."

I can't look at him. "Yeah."

"And you promise to tell me where you'll be next time? The truth?"

"Sure, Dad."

"Then I don't think we need to talk about punishment." He cuffs my shoulder a little too hard and stands up. "Hit the books, okay?"

I don't want to hit the books. I just want to go back to last night and skip that party. I want to invite Solstice over for scary movies and popcorn instead. Better yet, I want to go back to Carbondale, where nobody ever tried to put me into any fucking Prom Bowl.

"Maybe we need to talk about extending your curfew," Dad muses.

"No."

"Are you sure? Now that you're spending time with a more social crowd, maybe midnight is too early for a weekend night."

"Midnight is fine. It won't happen again."

"Well, if it does, honey, you just call me. We can make exceptions."

"Okay, Dad."

He leaves and I feel a hard weight settle in my gut.

It's not until English Lit on Monday morning that I finally hear about Solstice. According to Ms. Hess, a "teen rager" party got out of control Friday night. The way she talks about the party, like it's some sort of mythical drug carnival, makes it impossible to take her seriously. It's not until I hear the phrase "near-fatality" that my brain grinds into gear, but my tongue feels halfway down my throat and I can't figure out how to ask the follow-up questions I need answers to.

Fortunately, I can count on Charlotte to not know what's going on. "Does that mean someone died?"

"It means some of you are very, very, lucky," Ms. Hess says, glaring around the room at various kids who probably were not even at the party. "Had the young woman in question died, very serious legal action would have been considered."

"Is anyone going to jail?"

"Who was it?"

"What did she nearly die of?"

"Anyone who knows anything about these events should see a member of the faculty," Ms. Hess says, ignoring the onslaught of questions. "It's important for the health and safety of all our students that we prevent this kind of thing from happening in the future. Now, please open your books to page two-eleven."

• • •

I catch up with Charlotte and Kylie in the hall after class. "What do we do?"

"Do?" Charlotte looks confused.

"They're going to want to question us, right? Everyone knows we're involved in Prom Bowl. Shouldn't we, I don't know, talk about it? Decide what we're going to say?"

Kylie looks at me like I'm a three-year-old she's tired of indulging. "Nobody's saying anything, Ava."

"But won't they ask what we know about Sol?"

Charlotte grabs my wrist and tugs me over to the bank of lockers. "Ava, keep your mouth shut."

"What?"

"No one knows it was a Prom Bowl party. Cody isn't going to tell. Solstice won't tell. No one needs to find out."

My scalp prickles. "Are you serious? You're still protecting the stupid fucking Prom Bowl?"

"There's no reason we all have to get in trouble."

"We could stop this thing, Charlotte. If I went to the principal right now and showed him the pictures on my phone, if I told him what that party really was—"

"You'd get prom cancelled."

"Maybe prom needs to be cancelled!"

"You'd be *dirt*, Ava, you'd be less than dirt. You would be Public Enemy *Numero Uno* at Patterson. And I'd hate you too." Her face is pinched. "I've done *everything* for you this year. You probably wouldn't even still be in Prom Bowl in the first place if it weren't for me. You certainly wouldn't be dating Mark."

"That isn't true."

"Oh please, like he'd ever have noticed you if you hadn't jumped seven rungs up the social hierarchy. You're not that cute. You don't go to parties. You aren't in any sports or clubs. How were you going to make friends without me? How was Mark *ever* going to notice you?"

"Shut up." I can't get any volume behind my voice. I can't breathe.

"If you ruin my senior prom," she says, taking another step closer so I can smell her sour yogurt breath, "I will *never* forgive you."

I find Dad in his classroom, grading papers. The fact that Patterson has cast my father as the statistics teacher is mind-blowing to me. He is the worst at math. He has to get an accountant to do our taxes for him, and he gave up helping me and Sean with our math homework when we hit long division. But the rule is that every coach has to have a teaching job too, and the thing about math is that all the answers are in the back of the book.

He looks up when I come in. "Hey, kid."

"Dad, do you have a minute?"

"Sure. Are you missing class? Do you need a note?" He holds up his pad of excused absence notes like he's showing me a homemade pie or something. He is so proud of that thing, I have to smile.

"It's okay. It's lunch."

"In my day we had lunch monitors."

"Why? What trouble were you getting into in the cafeteria?"

"Food fights, mainly."

"Dad, did you go to high school in a family film from the eighties?"

"Hush."

I scuff my sneaker on the linoleum. "Did you hear about the girl?"

"The girl?"

"The one who got into trouble at the party. They told us about it in homeroom."

"Ahh." He sets his pen down. "Did that upset you, honey?"

"Of course."

"We're not allowed to release any names." By the way he's looking at me, though, I can tell he knows it was Solstice. My friend. "Kids are always going to make mistakes, you know? It sounds like that girl had too much to drink."

"Yeah."

"I'm just glad you weren't involved."

"Dad, the thing is—"

"Senior parties are like that sometimes, honey," he cuts me off. "It's an unpredictable environment. Sometimes it's unsafe. That's why I'm so glad I can count on you to make good choices and stay out of bad situations."

Does he really think I wasn't at the same party as Solstice? How many parties does he think there are on one Friday night? "Dad," I try, "you know the Prom Bowl?"

"Sure, honey."

"A lot of kids are saying—I mean, do you think there might be some connection?"

"Between what?"

"Prom Bowl and what happened to—the girl."

"What? Ava, no, Prom Bowl is a school-sponsored activity. It takes place on school grounds. The faculty know all about it."

"Are you sure?" I hold my breath. This is exactly what Charlotte just finished warning me about. If she knew I was here . . .

"Of course. Hell, I bought my date in the Prom Bowl when I was a senior. I remember how it was."

Well, that's gross.

"Just ignore the rumors, Ava. And don't spread them, okay? That kind of thing really upsets people, and we're new in town. I know you're leaving for college in a few months, but me and Sean, we have a future here to think about."

"I'm not . . . spreading rumors, Dad. I'm talking to *you*."

"During school hours I'm your teacher. I have a responsibility to stay impartial about things like this."

What the hell? "You're not my teacher. I'm not in Stats. And what are you saying, that you're not my dad when we're at school?"

"Ava, don't be childish."

"How am I being childish?"

"I'm depending on you to squash these rumors, not perpetuate them. Do you think that girl wants to be talked about behind her back?"

"But Dad, if it's the truth—"

"That's enough." He catches my gaze and holds it. "Ava, you understand that as Mark's coach, I'd have to take action if I felt he was involved in anything inappropriate."

I can't speak.

"You don't want to jeopardize Mark's scholarship chances, do you?"

No, I don't.

"Or my job?"

Dad.

"Whatever happened at that party, whatever bad judgment those kids showed, it's behind us now." Dad turns his focus back to the papers on his desk. "I don't want to discuss it anymore."

He gestures toward the pressed clay dish he keeps on his desk, a souvenir from my first-grade art class. I can still see my tiny thumbprints preserved in the sides. "Take a piece of candy," he urges, and I recognize my dismissal.

"I'm good," I tell him, because I know it's the only thing he really wants to hear from me.

16

Ava

I have gym next, thank God—no Prom Bowl girls and no Mark. I vent my rage on the badminton court, imagining that I'm ramming shot after shot down Cody's stupid smug throat. In reality, I suck at badminton, and the game consists of a lot more running after the birdie than aggressively scoring points. Still, by the end of the hour I'm tired and sweaty and those are really the only unpleasant things I'm thinking about.

The bell rings, signaling the end of the period. Fuck, Mr. Rodgers shorted us on our changing time again. I pick up the pace, already resigned to the fact that I'm going to be late for History. By the time I make it back to my gym locker, virtually everyone else from my class is gone and the next hour's class is making their way in. The configuration of people around open lockers is unfamiliar, and at first I don't recognize mine.

What clues me in is my purple empire top. My mom sent it to me the last time Sean visited her—packed it in his suitcase before putting him on the Greyhound back to us. I seriously considered never wearing it out of spite, but it looks awesome on me, so I usually try to pretend it was a gift from Sean. It's actually become one of my favorite shirts. I'd know it anywhere.

I'd even know it balled up on the floor with the muddy print of someone's sneaker across the back.

And that's when I notice that my locker is hanging open, empty, and that the rest of my clothes, my books, and my purse are all strewn out across the floor.

Kids are giving the whole situation a wide berth, cutting their gazes and their paths off to the side. I feel sick at the thought of collecting my things. It feels like an admission. If I acknowledge that I was a target, I'm saying that I deserved it. I was disliked. I was offensive. I was obnoxious or cruel or boring or . . . there are a million reasons kids go for each other like this, and they're all flashing through my mind like a vindictive slideshow. *What did I do? What's wrong with me?*

You're the Wild Card. Even your boyfriend does this shit to you.

I drop to my knees and sweep my things into a pile, trying to assess the damage as I go. I don't have any choice but to put on the muddy shirt, but maybe if I can get enough of the gunk off, I can wear it inside out and no one will notice.

My hand closes around something hard. My phone. I put it in my purse before class. Whoever did this would have had to go through my purse to find it. Now the screen is shattered and the back's ripped off, and I can tell at a glance that it's never going to work again.

"Ava?"

"One second." My vision's blurring. I don't want to cry, not now, but if I have to talk I'm not going to have any choice in the matter.

"Ava." Someone's kneeling down in front of me. "Shit, she really got you."

"I'm okay." I finally look up and see that it's Denise who's beside me. Someone from Prom Bowl is actually being nice to me. I could hug her. God, Denise is probably the only friend I have right now.

"We didn't think she'd really do it. Let me help, okay?"

"Who?"

"This whole thing has gotten out of hand. We were just talking about it at lunch. Charlotte's lost her shit entirely."

"What?"

"She told me and Olivia she was going to get your phone—"

"Charlotte, as in my *cousin* Charlotte?"

"She said you had pictures of that party and she had to get rid of them or something."

I run my thumb across the mutilated electronic mess of my phone. All the photos of the party are gone. All the photos of me and Mark are gone. All the texts he's ever sent me . . .

Not that I care, because Mark turned out to be a jerk like the rest of them. It doesn't matter. *Don't think about it.*

"This Prom Bowl shit has to stop," Denise says.

I breathe once, slowly. "What do we do?"

"I don't think we can *do* anything."

"We should go to the principal."

She grabs my shoulder. "We can't."

"Why? Why can't we?" I demand.

"Well . . . you know. Most people are on Charlotte's side. Even Solstice is."

How *can* she be? "Denise, my brother's going to be a senior in a few years."

"So's my sister. What's your point?"

"What if she ends up in the Bowl? What if in three years your sister's parading around half naked trying to get my little brother to buy her? You can't tell me you want that."

"We can't do it this way." She gets up off the floor and sits on the bench, and I join her. "Charlotte really has it in for you, Ava."

"I didn't even do anything to her."

"I don't know what her problem is. Maybe she's bugged that you're doing so well in the rankings. I know she's your cousin, but she doesn't exactly love it when people are more popular than her. Back in September, she started a rumor that this one girl had chlamydia."

"That cheerleader?"

"Laura Baretta."

"I heard about that!" I recall Charlotte's squeals of delight. She must have been excited that her rumor had made it back to her. "That wasn't true?"

"Not even kind of."

"How do you know?"

"She was dating my stepbrother at the time. Apparently

Charlotte told him, so he confronted Laura. She denied it, but by then the story was everywhere."

"Why would she do something like that?"

"People do fucked up shit to get a crown."

"We have to stop this. We have to go to the principal."

"No, you need to watch your step." Denise puts a hand on my arm. "You're already a target, Ava. She'll come after you. And don't think she'll be the only one. She hit Laura with that VD rumor just to keep her out of the Prom Bowl. What do you think she'll do to you if you get prom *cancelled*? And what do you think will happen to your little brother after you graduate, when we're the only school in Minnesota without a prom and everyone's looking for someone to blame? Who do you think is gonna take the heat? You won't be here."

I want to argue, to insist that no one would hurt Sean. I want to believe nobody would.

But I can't. Because now I'm remembering Mark's football banquet and meeting up with Sean after it ended, noticing spots of blood on his collar and the way he pulled on a hoodie over his button-down shirt before Dad could see. He'd whispered to me in the car that he'd had a bloody nose. Sean's never gotten bloody noses.

And I'm remembering Mark coming inside, quiet and distant, vague when I asked him where he'd been.

And Cody at the next table with his rumpled shirt and loosened tie. Like he'd been in a fight.

"You're right," I say softly. "I won't say anything."

17

Mark

I make my way to the office, barely breathing. It feels like the walls are watching me. The administration knows the Prom Bowl is connected to the party. Why else would they call me to the principal's office? I'm going to be kicked off the football team. I'm going to be expelled. They'll call Notre Dame and I'll lose my scholarship. Mom and Dad are going to be heartbroken. I'll have to go to community college and become a salesman and twenty years from now I'll be sitting in an office that smells like antiseptic and carpet cleaner, pushing papers around and wondering what happened to my life.

The secretary looks up when I walk in. She's missing her usual smile. "Mr. Palmer. You can go on through, he's expecting you."

Mr. Palmer. I'm always "Mark" to her. She scolds me with a smile when I'm late and have to come in for a note, and congratulates me when the honor roll sheet is posted. She likes me. She always has.

I keep walking.

The two armchairs facing Dr. Landau's desk are already

occupied, as is the bench. "Oh," I say, "I'm sorry, should I—?"

The girl on the bench turns. It's Solstice. She's hunched in on herself like she's trying to disappear, arms pulled up inside the sleeves of her giant sweater. She makes eye contact with me and then looks away.

I want to ask her if she's okay, but I am terrified that it might be somehow incriminating, so I say nothing and hate myself for it.

"Have a seat, Mr. Palmer," says Dr. Landau, gesturing to the bench. Solstice slides over a little to make room.

"Am I in trouble?" Oh good, Mark, that's something a guy who didn't do anything wrong would say.

Dr. Landau seems to have the same thought. "Should you be?"

"I mean . . . what's this regarding?" Now I sound like some kind of executive assistant, good Christ.

"Miss Downing and her parents are here to discuss some concerns they have about the events that occurred this past weekend."

"You mean the party?" I see no point in pretending I don't know about it. Dozens of people saw me there.

"That's right. The Downings have brought some serious allegations to our attention, and the school will be investigating. But I wanted to meet with you first."

"Why me?"

"You've always been an upstanding member of the Patterson community. You're the president of the student council, and that gives you some responsibility." He leans forward, elbows on his desk, and stares like he's trying to pull secrets out through my eyes. "What can you tell me about the party?"

"It was at Cody Spencer's house."

"We're aware of that. What else?"

"Some kids were drinking. There was a keg."

"Were you drinking?"

"No sir."

"He wasn't," Solstice says.

"Be quiet, Solstice," the woman in the chair speaks for the first time. Solstice's mother, I assume. She sounds like she's already told Solstice to be quiet several times, like she's tired of having to say it. It reminds me of Cody's mom when we were kids, telling him to sit down or stop playing with his spaghetti, asking him why he couldn't be more like me. Maybe that was another reason we usually played at my house.

"Ask him about this contest," Solstice's father says.

"We'll get there," Dr. Landau says.

"Solstice has been taking part in some competition all year, and we know this Spencer boy is behind it."

"Mr. Downing, please let me handle this."

"I want to know what really went on at that party. I know it was related to this—this *Prom Bowl*. I want Mr. Spencer and his friends held accountable!"

"Dad," Solstice tries, "it was just a regular party. It wasn't a Prom Bowl thing."

"She's covering for him," Mr. Downing growls. He stabs a finger at me. "Ask this one."

"Solstice has never been in trouble a day in her life," her mother chimes in. "She's a good girl. She doesn't drink. She's responsible. Something's behind this aberrant behavior."

Dr. Landau raises his eyebrows at me. "Mark?"

"Sir?"

"Did the party have anything to do with the Prom Bowl?"

For some reason I can't keep the memory of Ava, half naked and shivering in my arms, from my mind. I didn't protect her that night. I stood in the back of the room and let my classmates abuse her. Of course she's angry. Of course she doesn't want me anymore. Who the fuck would? I'm no upstanding member of the Patterson community. I'm a guy who watches girls get pushed around because I'm too scared or too stupid to intervene.

And Cody thinks I run this school. I don't run shit. I can't even prevent my girlfriend from being assaulted right the fuck in front of me.

Dr. Landau is waiting for an answer, and fuck the stupid prom, I want to tell him the truth. I want to tell him everything. At the very least, I can make sure what happened to Ava and Solstice doesn't happen to anybody else.

But I'll lose Notre Dame. Maybe I'll lose college altogether. Will anybody want me after the truth about my involvement in this comes out? All my parents' hopes for me, all their hard work—

it'll be wrecked. Do I really need to blow up my whole future over this? Is that my penance?

I can't do it.

"No," I tell Dr. Landau, feeling as spineless as a sunbaked jellyfish. "Like Solstice said, it was just a party."

Dr. Landau doesn't push, because of course he doesn't. No one wants to hear anything less than glowing about the Prom Bowl, do they? "Mr. Downing, the competition you're referring to is our annual prom fundraiser. It all takes place here on campus with faculty oversight. In fact, several of our alumni faculty took part when they were students. It's just a bit of harmless fun."

Solstice nods her agreement.

Is this some kind of cover-up? Or is Dr. Landau really this clueless?

"Mr. Palmer, you're excused. Please return to class." He scribbles a note on an attendance slip pad and tears it off for me. "If you do think of anything else you'd like to share about the party, feel free to come see me."

"Yes sir."

As I step out of the office, the bell—which isn't really a bell, but an institutional beep—goes off, signaling the end of a class period. The hall goes from zero to jam-packed in seconds as students embrace their five minutes of freedom between classes.

Murph Williams staggers by under a load of textbooks nearly as tall as he is. I catch him by the back of his collar. "Hey Murph."

"Hey Mark."

"What's with the library? You hiding a Time-Turner under your shirt?"

"Huh?"

"Not a reader?" I pluck the top book off his pile. "AP Statistics, huh? And *The Old Man and the Sea*?"

"Yeah."

"We're reading that in Senior AmLit. What are you doing with it?"

"It's not mine."

"So whose is it?"

"Brad Lennox. He asked me to carry it," Murph adds quickly, like he's afraid I'm going to bust him for textbook stealing.

I glance around the hall and spot Brad, propped up with a hand against the wall and leaning in toward a girl who looks about Murph's age. She giggles at something he says and looks away, and then, in full view of the fucking main office, he slides a hand down and cups her ass.

Something inside me tears.

I grab the top two books off of Murph's pile, stalk across the hall, and pull Brad off the girl. "Go to class," I tell her, and she scampers off like a possum in the headlights.

"Dude!" Brad protests.

I shove the books into his chest. Hard. He staggers back. "Carry your own fucking books, Lennox. You have arms."

"What the *hell* is your problem?"

"Beat it."

"Asshole," Brad spits.

I need to get out of here. I need to leave this shit behind and go to Indiana and start over.

As I turn to leave, I see Ava on the stairs, her head sticking up above the thinning crowd. She's watching me. I make my way over. "Hey."

"Hi." Her tone is cold.

"I—how are you?"

"Fine."

"How's Sean?"

"Ask him yourself."

"Ava, I didn't know he was going to be at—"

"I really don't want to talk about that with you." She steps away from me and blinks hard, twice. It's so familiar. It's so *Ava*. She's trying not to cry.

Oh, Ava.

I so want to take her hand, pull her into my arms so she can hide the fact that she's crying. Instead, she swallows hard and her eyes clear. She sets her jaw. "Did you know they trashed my gym locker?"

"What? Who did?"

"Charlotte. Maybe some others." She fishes her phone out of her pocket and holds it up for my inspection. It's totaled. Shit.

"It's fucked," I say. "I know it is. That's why I—I don't know if you saw—Brad was making Murph Williams carry his—"

"I saw it."

"I'm not going to let that fly anymore."

"Do you want a medal?"

"No, I just—"

"Like you're some kind of noble avenger, protecting kids from having to carry the books of bigger kids?" She shakes her head. "Like that solves anything?"

"Ava . . ."

"Were you in the meeting today with Solstice and her parents?"

"How did you know about that?"

"I saw them going into the office earlier. And I just saw you come out. It wasn't hard to put it together." She takes a shuddery breath. "They wouldn't even let her talk to me."

"Ava—"

"*Were* you in the meeting?"

"Yeah."

"Did you tell them? About the Prom Bowl and everything?"

She would have forgiven me. I can see it in her eyes. If I'd done the right thing in there, if I had stopped worrying about covering my own ass and been honest about what was going on, she would have forgiven me. Even after everything that's happened.

"No." I can't look her in the eye.

"Typical."

"I'm sorry."

"I know you are," she says resignedly.

I can't think of what else to say. Maybe there isn't anything.

"I have to get to class," she says, and steps around me, leaving me alone in the hall.

Ava

"Solstice! *Sol!*"

Seeing her here, in the fluorescent lighting of the hallway with kids milling all around her, is surreal. The last time I saw Solstice, she was unconscious on the floor of Cody's bathroom.

She looks like maybe she hasn't slept since then. Her eyes are bloodshot and her face is broken out, and frizzy curls are escaping from her ponytail. She's in sweatpants and sneakers. "Hey," she says.

"You're back?"

"Just for my stuff." She reaches into her open locker and pulls out a handful of assorted refuse—pens, pencils, lip gloss, thumb drive. It all goes into her backpack. "My parents are waiting in the parking lot."

I don't get it. "Waiting for what?"

"I'm leaving."

"Leaving?"

"They're taking me out of school."

"They can't do that. You haven't graduated!"

"They say I'll enroll at St. Benedict's and finish the year there."

"What's that, Catholic school?"

"Yeah."

"You aren't Catholic."

"Doesn't matter. They don't want me at Patterson anymore."

"Why not?"

She slams her locker door and faces me. "Don't be a dumbass, okay?"

"I'm not!"

"The school closed the investigation into the party. That's why not."

"I didn't know that, Solstice. How was I supposed to know that?"

"Sure." She turns away.

I grab her arm. "I *didn't*."

"Your dad works for the school."

"Well, he didn't tell me."

"Your boyfriend was the one who convinced them to drop it."

"I don't *have* a boyfriend."

She raises her eyebrows.

"Anyway, I thought . . . Charlotte told me you were protecting Cody. She said you were going to say the party had nothing to do with Prom Bowl."

"Yeah. But *someone* is obviously spreading a different story around, because my parents are just *convinced* there's a connection."

"You don't seriously think I told your parents."

"I think you said something to somebody and word got around. Everyone knows you took pictures, Ava."

They do? "I don't have them anymore."

"Maybe you do and maybe you don't. But the only reason to take pictures at all would be to get us all in trouble."

"Solstice, you didn't like Prom Bowl either, you thought it was stupid. . . ."

"But I can handle my shit! Cody Spencer didn't make me get up in front of the entire senior class and drink my weight in cheap beer. The Prom Bowl didn't make me do it. I just fucking did it. And that's on me. So yeah, I had a wicked hangover and a head injury. I got suspended, I deserved that. But now I'm going to have to finish my senior year in Jesustown with a bunch of strangers because *you* were more interested in playing *CSI* than in staying with me while I was passed out in a fucking bathroom."

I lean against the wall.

None of this is anything I haven't been thinking since that night, is the thing.

Solstice had a head wound.

I left her.

She was stupid and wrong and made some fucked up choices.

But I left her.

"Ava, you don't want to get prom cancelled," Solstice says, and her voice is gentle. It's like she needed to hit me to wake me up, and she knows it was effective. All the anger's just gone. "Getting prom cancelled doesn't fix this."

"Does anything fix this?"

"Probably not." She barks out a laugh.

"I don't want my little brother to have to do this in three years."

"Do you want your little brother to be known as the guy whose sister got prom cancelled?"

"Are those my only choices? God, Sol."

"Most people aren't involved in Prom Bowl," she says. "But everyone goes to prom."

Yeah. "I can't believe you're leaving."

"Me either."

"Are you going to be okay, Sol?"

"Physically? I feel like I could sleep until the next apocalypse."

"Not just physically."

"No," she says, simply.

"I'm sorry. Fuck. I'm so sorry."

"This has really trashed my life," she says. "But at the end of the day . . . you know, I was doing it because I wanted to. I wanted to win it. I couldn't admit it before, but I did."

"You probably would have," I tell her.

She shakes her head. "At this point? You better win, Ava. I don't think I'll be able to stand it if it's anyone else."

Impulsively, I hug her. "I'll see you around."

But I don't believe I will.

18

Mark

After my confrontation with Ava, there's only one person in the world I want to talk to. We may not be on good terms, but we've been best friends for years, and I'm hoping that fact still means more than all the other shit that's gone down this year.

I have to ring the doorbell three times before Cody's mom comes to the door. She looks like she's aged about ten years since the last time I saw her. Normally, Mrs. Spencer is impeccably coiffed, but today I guess she's going for more of an Art Garfunkel situation. I very actively do not stare.

"Cody's grounded," she says shortly. It's clear whatever standing I've had in the past as Cody's good-influence friend is gone. She definitely knows I was at the party.

"I just need to see him for a few minutes. Please."

She side-eyes me for a moment. "Fifteen minutes then."

"Thanks, Mrs. Spencer."

I take the stairs two at a time. Cody's room is at the end of the long upstairs hall, and it's massive, more than twice the size of mine. We never played here as kids. We were so small, and the space was so big, that somehow our games never seemed to fill it. Our fantasy worlds were in corners of the backyard, in the sandbox his father built, in trees with branches we could reach. Never here.

I knock once.

Cody opens the door with the kind of surly expression that can only have been intended for his mother. It drops from his face when he sees me. "Oh."

"Hey."

"What are you doing here?"

"Can I come in?"

"I'm grounded. Pending formal charges."

"Yeah, your mom let me up. Obviously."

He shrugs. "Whatever."

All the seating in Cody's room is designed to make you comfortable, at ease. He doesn't have a desk chair. He has a beanbag and a couple of butterfly chairs, all set up around his flatscreen. I don't want to be comfortable. I stay standing.

Cody drops into the beanbag chair, clearly waiting for me to speak first. I'm not going to. "What's up?" he says finally.

"About the party."

"Christ, not you too."

"What the fuck *was* that?"

"It was a drink-off, Palmer, you've seen them before."

"Don't fuck with me."

"Fine, let's get to it then. What did you *really* come here to ask me?"

I swallow hard. "I want to know why you bullied my girlfriend into stripping in front of the entire senior class."

"I didn't bully her."

"You called her a bitch, dude. You hurt her."

"She *is* a bitch, Mark."

"You'd better watch it."

"Yeah? Or else what?"

This is not my best friend.

Cody's looking at me like he doesn't recognize me either. "Are you going to hit me again?"

"You deserve it." I have no idea whether I mean that or not.

"Ava's been trying to take down Prom Bowl from the beginning," he says. "She's a fucking—"

"Careful."

"*—malcontent.*"

"Why should she be content? We made her auction herself off to the highest bidder, Cody. You don't think that's twisted?"

"I think that's *the game*. Nobody takes this seriously, man. The girls all go to prom and dance with whoever they want to anyway. There's no way to enforce the bidder's rights. It's just a silly goddamn tradition that some of us happen to like. And you've been freaking out all year because the new girl can't wrap her head around it."

"It doesn't matter if you think it's silly. She shouldn't have to do it."

"She doesn't have to derail the whole fucking event just because she doesn't want to play."

"She's not trying to derail it, Cody. She's trying to get out of it."

"And I wish *you* would just stay the hell out of it."

"She's my girlfriend!"

"She was my Wild Card *first*!"

He's standing now, heaving like a disgruntled toddler, and it strikes me how ridiculous he's being. Offensive and insensitive, sure, but also just goddamn ridiculous. "Are you saying you had a prior claim?"

"Well, I did."

"Jesus, are you even listening to yourself?"

"You're such a fucking showboat, Mark."

"What does *that* mean?"

"Everything's all about you. You you you. Mark Fucking Palmer, boy wonder, magical quarterback with a four-point-oh and a heart of gold."

"I don't have a four-point-oh; I got a B in Pre-Calc."

"Well fucking wait here while I get you a pillow to cry into."

"Cody, what the hell is your problem?"

"Prom Bowl was *my* thing! Everybody knows the senior class president is a fucking figurehead, but this was my chance to do something people cared about. And I *worked* on it. You can stand here and say it's stupid because you weren't up all night coming up with events people would want to do, and setting up the Facebook page and organizing the bidding and everything. You run around on the field and people throw money at you and everyone loves you, and I've been doing my best to make this awesome and everyone's just all pissed off now."

"Cody—"

"I *knew* you liked her, okay? I mean, I always knew."

This admission catches me by surprise. "How?"

"Dude, you haven't been serious about a girl the entire time we've been at Patterson. I'm not blind."

"I asked you not to Wild Card her." But, holy shit, what if I hadn't? What if I hadn't brought her to his attention that night at the season opener? Would Cody have left Ava alone?

"Yeah, that was kind of a giveaway right there," he confirms.

"So then why did you do it?"

"I don't know. I was pissed at you. We always talked about how we were going to rule this place during senior year, but you were doing it without me. You were all, star-of-the-team, student-council-president, chatting-up-the-new-girl, and meanwhile Coach Vanguard didn't even know my name. And then you were trying to boss me around about the one thing that was actually *mine*."

Shit. "I didn't want to do it without you, man. I'm sorry if that's how it looked."

"That's how it *was*. Doesn't matter whether you meant it or not."

I sit down in a butterfly chair. "Not like we planned it, huh."

"It's whatever."

"Come on, don't be like that."

"You got the girl and the fancy scholarship and I got suspended. The end."

"I didn't get the girl."

"What?"

"We're broken up, I think."

"Who ended it?"

"I don't know. Both of us. Or neither of us. It was weird."

"Oh. That blows."

It's not very sincere, but it's something. "You could still get a scholarship," I say, after a pause.

He snorts. "No one gives a scholarship to a second-string player who never gets off the bench. I haven't even gotten any offers."

"Did you send letters of interest?"

"Spit in the wind."

"I'm sorry." And I really am, but I am also aware that Cody doesn't need a scholarship the way I do. This Taj Mahal of a bedroom does not belong to a kid who needs financial assistance. Cody's going to college, he's just not going to be a football player.

Maybe I'm not the one who needs a pillow to cry into.

Or maybe this was never about football. Maybe this is about the plans and dreams of two ten-year-old kids in a tree fort, and the fact that they aren't coming true. Maybe all of this is because I wasn't careful with my best friend and he wasn't careful with me. And now we've created a gap that no apology can bridge.

Maybe I'm just a goddamn idiot who isn't careful with the

people I love in general—and suddenly the fact that I can't go to prom with Ava matters so much less than the knowledge that she can't even look me in the eyes.

"What happens now?" I ask Cody.

"Final bidding for Prom Bowl's still on."

"You sure that's what you want to do?"

"Doesn't matter what I want, does it?" He shrugs. "We both know you're going to call the play, Mark. You always do."

19

Ava

I remember winter break being magical when I was a kid. It seemed huge, a vacation on the scale of summer, with the added bonus of Christmas in the middle. My mom gave us low-key celebrations on our birthdays—dinner at our favorite restaurant and a gift or two—but for Christmas she pulled out the big guns. The house in Carbondale smelled like evergreen and warm apple pie from Black Friday until New Year's. And on Christmas morning, Sean and I were under strict instructions to stay in our rooms until she called us to come and see what Santa had left. The whole Santa Claus thing went on way longer than was age-appropriate, and the fat man was always excessively generous. We'd be opening presents until noon.

Last year, the first Christmas without her, none of us were really up for the hoopla. Dad made his famous chili and we went to see an action movie. Sean and I exchanged presents. Dad gave us each Amazon gift cards.

I was going to suggest doing it right this year. Maybe not the old grandiosity, but we could get a tree and bake a ham, or at least order one. I'd received my college letters a week ago—accepted at University of Illinois, Southern Illinois, University of Minnesota, Minnesota State, and, surprisingly, UCLA—and felt like doing something as a family to celebrate. But then Sean announced he was going to spend the holiday with Mom.

I don't know why I'm surprised by anything anymore.

"She cares more about Christmas than Dad does," Sean says. We're sitting in the den, pretending to watch TV. "She's religious," he adds, reading my mind.

"You're not religious."

"That's not the point, Ave."

"What's the point then?"

"It's *Mom*."

I don't know how to roll my eyes hard enough at that.

"She wants to see you too," he says.

"She knows where I live."

"Come on, she can't come here. Her and Dad under one roof?"

"They lived under one roof for years."

"Which was a terrific success."

"It was fine until she bailed."

"She didn't bail for no reason."

"What's that supposed to mean?"

"Dad can be difficult, you know that."

"She didn't just leave Dad," I say. "She left you too, you know. You're telling me you're fine with that?"

"I'm just saying everybody screws up."

"That's one hell of a screw-up."

"Yeah. But she's still Mom."

My new phone vibrates in my pocket. The one good thing about Charlotte's locker attack was getting an upgrade. The message is from an unknown number: Final Prom Bowl auction closes March 1st 4pm sharp place yr bids ASAP. I can't even get away from it during winter break. I chuck my phone at the wall.

Sean stares. "You trying to break your phone again?"

"Stupid Prom Bowl. I just . . ." I am *not* about to start crying in front of my baby brother over a text message, my God.

"It's almost over," Sean says. "You don't have to do anything else, even."

"What are you talking about?"

"Your part's over. All the events. You can just ignore the whole thing at this point, really."

"I can't ignore it, Sean, they're bidding on *me*. I'm not done. I have to go to prom with whoever wins."

"So you have to go to prom. What's the big deal? You were probably going to go anyway, right?"

"Are you serious?"

"I just don't know why you're so upset. You've been this way for months and I don't get it."

"Well, how would you like it? How would you feel if all the girls at Patterson got together and decided how much they'd be willing to pay for a date with you? And then you actually had to go on that date? When all you really wanted was to hang out with the one fun, cool person who seemed like they liked you for real, and who you really liked too? How would you like it?"

He shrugs. "I . . . I don't think I'd care."

"You wouldn't *care*?"

"It's just one night. It's like how the older guys on the football team get to give us a hard time this year because we're the freshmen. It's annoying, but it's temporary. And next year I'll be on the other side and some kid will have to carry *my* lunch tray and inspect *my* cleats for spiders before I put them on."

"Did you really have to do that?"

"Ever since one of the guys found a wolf spider sneaking out of his shoe, yeah."

"Gross."

"No kidding."

"When you're an upperclassman, will you also make your freshmen serve drinks at parties where girls take their clothes off?"

He squirms. "I mean, I wouldn't host that party. So . . ."

"I'm never going to be on the other end of it," I tell him. "That's the difference. The guys at Patterson do this to the girls and then everybody just *leaves*. We don't have a chance to do it back to them. Everyone wants to act like the Prom Bowl is a fun tradition that everybody loves to do, but nobody asked me if I wanted to, and when I said I didn't, they told me I had to. And there is nothing at all in it for me."

He's quiet. On screen, the Grinch is stealing the last can of Who Hash.

"If it's so much fun," I say, "you should get them to reverse it. Next year. Or when you're a senior. Have the contestants be guys for a change. See if everyone still enjoys it when it's like that. Maybe you could be a contestant."

"Ave."

"What."

"You know you sound like Mom?"

"I do not."

"That's exactly the kind of thing she used to say to Dad. When he missed stuff because of football, she'd tell him he'd never make it as a single parent. Remember?"

"I don't think he ever thought it was a serious threat, though."

Sean looks down at his phone, not typing. "You know, for whatever it's worth, I don't think she'd have let you do the Prom Bowl."

"You think?"

"She's strict."

"Yeah."

"I used to hate that."

"Same." I grab the remote and switch off the movie. I don't want to watch the part where the Grinch's heart grows three sizes. It always makes me cry. "Come on," I tell my brother. "I'll help you pack."

• • •

It's annoying, but it's temporary. I try to keep my brother's words in mind as I navigate the first day back at school. Sean isn't here. He's in Carbondale, still, because Dad holds practices on Monday nights and didn't want to drive down and pick him up until Tuesday. They'll get a hotel, I'm sure, and drive back on Wednesday, which means I'm on my own tomorrow and Sean won't be in school until Thursday.

I'm holding my breath as I approach my locker, imagining all kinds of sabotage, but it's intact. I spin the combination and open it, and there are all my books and binders, lined up the way I left them. Still, the building's been deserted for two weeks and it's hard to trust that anyone's going to leave me alone now that we're back. I empty everything important into my backpack, slam my locker shut, and spin the lock. Good luck, Charlotte.

I hurry to English Lit and get there before almost anyone else. Unfortunately, Ms. Hess assigns seats, so I can't isolate myself in a corner or even choose a spot that isn't directly in front of my arch nemesis, but I do have time to set up a subtle defensive play. Starting at the end of our column of chairs, I slide each one back to create extra space between them. I do the same thing starting at the front of the column, increasing the gaps. The students who beat me to class watch me like I'm a TV crime special, but I don't care. The chairs are spaced too far apart for Charlotte to mess with me during class without being obvious about it. I sit at my own desk and test my theory, aiming a kick at the seat in front of me. I can't reach it.

Okay.

Charlotte comes in, chatting with Laura Baretta. Head Cheerleader Laura, she of the chlamydia rumor. I guess they're friends again. I wonder if Laura knows who started the rumor about her, if she's just so relieved to no longer be public enemy number one that she's willing to overlook Charlotte's crap. That's a depressing thought.

On the way to her seat, Charlotte rests a hand on top of my copy of *A Farewell to Arms*. "Good Christmas, Ava?"

What's her game? "It was okay."

She waits. "Aren't you going to ask about mine?"

She's talking loud. She wants an audience. I'm supposed to embarrass myself. I meet her gaze instead. "How was your Christmas?"

"Really great. Mom took me dress shopping." She stresses the word "Mom."

Yeah, classy. "That's great, Char."

"Got your prom dress yet?"

"I haven't decided if I'm going."

"You're so funny, Ava." She bares her teeth in something that isn't a smile and moves on.

For the rest of the day I'm on high Charlotte alert. Fortunately, our paths don't organically cross again except at lunch, and it's easy enough to spend the hour in the library messing around on the Internet. With ten minutes to go until the next period starts, I scarf my falafel and stuffed grape leaf in the hidden corner of the stairwell. I'm so focused on sating my hunger that I don't even recognize the voice echoing down from above me at first. When I realize who it is, I eat the rest of my grape leaf in one bite and head for the exit before he can see me. I'll take the other stairs up to the second floor, even though it's out of my way. I'd way rather get a little exercise than face Cody Spencer.

Then I catch what he's saying. "Only the hottest girls get to go to prom as sophomores, you know."

"Uh-huh," comes the breathy response.

"You'd like to go, wouldn't you?"

"Yeah."

I can't move. I'm rooted to the spot. Is Cody Spencer seriously asking a girl barely older than my brother to prom? The same Cody Spencer who, just a few weeks ago, made me and my friends prove we'd be worthy prom dates by getting drunk and naked?

"Do you think we'd have a good time?" Cody's voice is disgustingly faux-innocent. It's like listening to Justin Bieber in the heart of his suck period. "I like to party," Cody adds. "Are you cool with that?"

"*So* cool," the girl assures him. "I can tell my mom I'm at my friend Jess's house."

Hang on, *Jess*? "Hey!" I call.

There's a moment of silence, and then a girl peeks over the railing and down at me. *Cassie.* Cassie who I met at the fashion show, Cassie who wanted to be like me. "Ava!"

"Hey Cass."

She ducks under Cody's arm and scampers down the flight of stairs. "Cody Spencer just asked me to prom, can you believe it?"

"Uh-huh. So I heard." I glare at Cody. "What the hell are you doing?"

"Easy, tiger." He laughs.

I totally get why Mark punched him. "I can't believe you're still doing this."

"Doing what, exactly?"

"Pushing people around."

"Who's pushing people around? She wants to go to the dance."

"She wants to get dressed up and go out for a nice dinner and dance with her friends. She doesn't want to go to some gross afterparty with you and the football team."

"Soured on football players, huh?"

"Oh my God, this is not about Mark, Cody."

"Suuuuure it isn't." Clearly the suspension had no effect on him. God, it's no surprise this messed-up tradition has been going on since Dad was in school.

Cassie steps forward and puts a hand on my arm. "Ava, I don't know what your problem with Cody is, but I'm fine. I *want* to go to prom. Please let this go."

I should tell her what Cody's capable of. I should tell her she's too good for him and always will be. But I can see in her eyes that she won't believe me. And even if she did, the truth wouldn't matter. Not when a date to senior prom is at stake. Before I can think of the words to convince her, Cassie rejoins Cody and they walk away together. I've missed my chance.

I didn't make a difference for this girl. I didn't make a difference for anyone. It was all bullshit, the whole time.

20

Mark

I've been refreshing my Facebook page for the past fifteen minutes, waiting for the auction results. I don't know why I'm doing this to myself. I don't have any money to put down on Ava. Not that she wants to go to prom with me anyway at this point. I've lost her. It's over.

Refresh. Refresh. Nothing.

Okay. I have to get out of the house.

My parents barely look up as I pass. Their eyes are fixed on the TV, where Notre Dame's basketball team is taking on Wake Forest. As I cross between them and the TV, I realize Mom's wearing a Notre Dame sweatshirt already.

No pressure then.

"Going out?" Dad calls.

"For a walk."

"Pretty cold out there."

"I have my coat."

"Don't stay out too late," Mom says.

The sun is already sinking below the treeline. I pull my hat down over my ears and hunch my shoulders against the wind. I always think people walking outside in winter look like they're marching to their own executions, all purposeful and downcast. Me, I couldn't be less purposeful. I have no idea where I'm going. There's the Dunkin' Donuts, but that's a hell of a walk and I only have three dollars in my pocket. Ordinarily I'd be going to Cody's, trying to get him on board for a couple of rounds of Call of Duty. But Cody and I haven't spoken since I confronted him about the party. Now that he's back in school, we avoid each other like charged ions.

Most of the guys aren't speaking to me, actually. It's weird. It's kind of hammering home the point that our time as a football team is over. I'm not the quarterback anymore, because we'll all be graduating before the new season opens and someone else will be in my position. And I'll be off at Notre Dame, probably (let's be honest) keeping their bench warm while an upperclassman gets all the playing time.

At least I'll be in the uniform. At least I'll be part of the team. I'll get to take the field, probably see some minutes when the first-string guy is tired or we're way ahead. I'll have my shot in a couple of years. And that isn't nothing. That's a hell of a lot more than Cody's getting.

I don't even register where my feet are taking me until I'm actually turning onto Ava's street. When I see where I am, I almost turn back. I can't imagine she wants to see me. We didn't even give each other the courtesy of a formal breakup. It was a game of chicken for days, waiting to see if either of us would change our Facebook status from "in a relationship" to "single." That status stuck around and mocked us, and every time I saw it I thought maybe I still had a shot, maybe things weren't ruined, maybe it wasn't over. And then I'd see Ava in the hall at school and she'd look at me like I was something she'd found dead in her yard. Finally I changed the Facebook status myself. I couldn't look at it anymore. I couldn't keep hoping.

I'm about to turn around for real and head home, but then I see her.

She's out in her yard, curled up in the hammock under a heavy blanket. It's the same blanket she and I cuddled under the night of our *Jurassic Park* marathon. She threw popcorn at the screen and heckled the Tyrannosaurus rex, and I loved her. We made out through most of the third movie. It was one of the best nights I can remember.

She looks up from the book in her hand and sees me. For a minute I think she might go inside, but then she lifts a hand in tentative greeting. An invitation, maybe?

I walk up the lawn and stand beside her. "Hey."

"Hi."

"What are you reading?"

"Raymond Chandler. I'm not reading it anymore. It's too dark out."

"Yeah."

"What are you doing here?"

"I was just out for a walk and . . . I don't know. I came here."

"To see me?"

"There wasn't really a plan."

"Gotcha."

"It's good," I add. "To see you."

"Yeah?"

"Of course."

"You too." She shifts over on the hammock a little. "You want to sit?"

I do. The hammock tilts to the side a bit as it takes my weight. Once we're stable, Ava pushes off with her feet and sets us swinging back and forth. I help out on the next push, since my legs are longer.

"How've you been?" she asks after a while.

"Okay. I mean, not great."

"You never got into trouble for the party, did you?"

"No."

"I figured."

"How about you?"

She's quiet for several swings. "I tried to tell my dad about it."

"What did he say?"

"It was like he didn't even hear me. He just told me not to go spreading rumors."

"Rumors?"

"No one wants to say it," she says. "No one wants to hear it."

"Hear what?"

"That the party was a Prom Bowl thing."

"Covering their asses."

"But he's my dad," she says. "He should be on my side."

"I'm sure he is, Ava."

"You weren't there. He wasn't even listening. Everything I said, he just warped it into what he wanted to hear. Do you know he offered to extend my curfew after the party? I mean, he didn't know where I was, but he knew I stayed out all night and lied to him about being at my aunt's, and all he did was ask if I needed a later curfew."

"At least you didn't get in trouble."

"I wish I had," she says. "It's like he doesn't even care what happens to me."

"Of course he cares."

"He doesn't act like it."

I put my arm around her. She stiffens for a minute, then relaxes into me. We never slept together, me and Ava. What a shitty thing to be thinking now, while she's so upset. But I'd forgotten how great she feels curled up against me.

"You know what Sean said?"

"What?"

"He said Mom wouldn't have let me do Prom Bowl."

"Is he right?"

She shivers a little. "I don't know. I haven't talked to her in over a year."

"Wow." I knew Ava was on bad terms with her mom, but I never realized it was that bad. I can't imagine not talking to one of my parents for that long. No matter how mad I got.

"Why did I do that?" she whispers, shivering again, and I realize she's crying. "Why did I stop talking to her?"

"She left you guys."

"Dad. She left Dad. She didn't leave me." She takes a ragged breath. "I left her."

I tighten my arm around her and just listen.

"I don't even know why she left," Ava says. "I made up reasons to explain it. I told myself she didn't care about us, she was cheating on Dad . . . but I don't know what happened. Sean goes to her for the holidays. I was always invited. She still wanted me. And Dad . . . he just doesn't *listen*, and if he doesn't listen to me, he probably didn't listen to her. Maybe she tried to tell him she was unhappy. Maybe she tried to make it work."

"You think it's his fault she left?"

"I'm just saying I don't know. I always assumed it was all her fault. And now I don't know. And I haven't spoken to her in over a year and she's my *mom,* so, like, shit, what if this was all a misunderstanding?"

"Call her," I say.

"I can't just—"

"Sure you can. It's your mom. She loves you no matter what's happened. Call her."

She nods into my neck. It feels like the way she used to nuzzle me between kisses, and God, I want to kiss her.

"How come you're not online, watching the auction?" she asks.

"I don't have anything to bid."

"Yeah, I figured you'd be with Cody, though. Doesn't he have to run it?"

"Yeah. I don't know. I think me and Cody are kind of over."

She sits up a little. "What? Why?"

"Because he's an ass. And because he doesn't listen either."

"Mmm, yeah."

"I swear he wasn't always like this."

"Are you okay?"

"I don't know. Not really. I miss him. But, like, not the guy he is now. The guy I started high school with. The guy I knew when we were kids."

"When did he change?"

"I have no idea. I didn't notice. I didn't notice until he was fucking attacking you at that party—fuck."

"That's not your fault."

"It doesn't matter if it's—"

My hip buzzes where it's pressed up against Ava.

I reach for it automatically, even though I never keep my phone in my side pocket. My hand bumps Ava's. "It's me," she says.

"What's up?"

She pulls out her phone and taps it awake. "Oh."

"What?"

"Auction's over."

I make a grab for my own phone, in the pocket of my jacket. Sure enough, I've got the same message from Cody: Auction results live. It must be a blast. Cody hasn't texted me in weeks.

"Should we check it?" I ask.

She shrugs. "Later."

"You don't care who won you?"

"They auctioned me off, Mark. The only person I ever wanted to go to prom with was you. I take it you didn't *win me*."

"No."

"So who cares?"

"I'm sorry," I say. "I should have gotten you out of it when you first asked me to. I'm so sorry."

"Then some other girl would have been dragged into it," she says.

"Maybe that girl would have wanted it, though."

"Yeah. Maybe." She sighs and reaches out with a toe to kick the ground, setting the hammock swinging again. "Maybe you weren't totally wrong, though. Maybe I did kind of want it. It was fun sometimes, feeling like part of something so . . ."

"Glamorous? Scandalous?"

"Significant."

"Ah."

"I'm sure you know the feeling," she says. "Quarterback Mark Palmer."

"Ava?"

"Hmm?"

"Would you still want to go to prom with me? If we had the choice?"

"What does it matter?"

"I don't know. Changes how I feel about it."

She disengages herself from my arm and sits up. "Yeah. I would."

"Even though we . . ."

"Broke up?"

"Well."

"It's not like we were going to last forever anyway," she says.

"What do you mean?"

"We're graduating in two months. And then we'll probably never see each other again."

"Jeez, downer."

"Not really. You were my high school boyfriend."

"That's all I was to you?" I don't know why I'm protesting. I didn't get into this expecting some big long-term thing, and I can't stand the idea of being one of those couples who exchange promise rings and go around saying they're "engaged to be engaged." But it still sucks to hear that she always saw us as a temporary thing.

"It isn't nothing," Ava says. "I mean . . . you know. You were my *first* boyfriend. You were my first kiss. When I think of senior year, I'm always going to think of you, even when I'm old and married and all that. Of course I wanted to go to prom with you. I wanted that memory with *you*, not some rando."

"You'll save me a dance, won't you?"

"Of course."

"So that's something."

"It isn't nothing."

The wind kicks up around us. It's the kind of early spring wind that isn't ready to admit winter is over, that bites through your clothes and stings your skin and chills your bones until they hurt. Ava squishes closer to me and I wrap the blanket tighter around us.

"You know, you're my best friend," I say into her hair.

She barks out a laugh. "That's convenient for you."

"Yeah, it is."

"Burn through one best friend, get another?"

"Hey."

"Sorry. That was mean." She takes a deep breath. "Mark?"

"Yeah?"

"I'm going to tell them."

"About the Bowl?"

"Yeah. All of it. What really happened at the party."

"You know that's why Cody got suspended, right?"

"So I'll get in trouble. Mark, I've been losing my mind for the last few months. I have to do something or I'm just going to flip out entirely."

"Solstice got suspended too," I remind her. "They won't let the other girls off the hook."

"No, well, why would they?"

"Arguably, because you guys are the victims?"

"I mean . . ." She pushes a hand through her hair. It gets stuck halfway in that thicket of curls. Ava's hair is deep and complex. "You'd have to make a really convincing argument. All of us were there voluntarily. No one did anything they didn't want to do."

"You're telling me you wanted to take your clothes off?"

"Well—"

"You were bullied into it."

"Okay, but—"

"But?"

"Okay. Yeah. You're right."

"And you're fine with being suspended for that?"

"I'd rather be suspended than keep my mouth shut and pretend it didn't fucking happen, all right? If the administration can't think of a better way to deal with it than to suspend me, that's their problem. And if it pisses you off or makes you think I'm being stupid or whatever, then that's *your* problem."

"Okay," I say. "Okay."

"I'm gonna tell Dr. Landau on Monday. And I'm going to see if I can spend spring break with my mom."

"Wow. Yeah?"

"If everyone here is about to hate me for being honest, I might as well leave the state," she says.

"I should do it."

"You should do what?"

"Be the one to tell."

"Mark."

"Fuck, I should. I'm the one who deserves to be suspended here."

"You'll lose your scholarship."

"Maybe I won't."

"With a suspension on your record?"

"I mean, I'm a pretty good quarterback."

Ava leans back into the hammock and takes me with her. "You were a really great high school boyfriend."

"Past tense."

"You'll always be my really great high school boyfriend," she says, and smiles.

21

Ava

Dad doesn't turn around when he hears me come into the kitchen. "Sunday breakfast, kid?"

I used to think it was endearing when he called me "kid." Now I sort of wonder whether he knows which of his kids I am. "Sure."

Sunday breakfast is basically leftovers—anything in our fridge and pantry that can masquerade as a morning meal. On good days it's a huge skillet full of eggs, cheese, meat, and vegetables. Today, though, it looks like Dad is making french toast out of stale sourdough and pan-frying some pepperoni pieces in lieu of bacon. I hold out my plate for a couple of slices.

"Smells good, huh?"

"Do we have syrup?"

"Butter and jam."

Of course. "Dad?"

"Eat up!"

"Can we talk?"

"What about?" He's got his back to me, whipping up more

toast to add to the gargantuan stack. No family of three, not even one containing my little brother, could possibly eat as much french toast as Dad is cooking.

"Can you stop doing that?" I ask. "Come sit down?"

He does. "Is everything okay?"

"I want to talk to you about the Prom Bowl."

"Did you win it?" He laughs at his own joke.

"I came in second."

"Did you really!"

"A girl called Caity won."

"Caity Pierce?"

"How do you know Caity Pierce?"

"She's one of my cheerleaders."

His cheerleaders? Gross gross gross, Dad.

"I'm not surprised," he says. "She's a cute girl. Very friendly."

And I'm not, I guess? Whatever.

As an afterthought, he says, "Second place. That's really something, Ava. That is something indeed."

"Thanks." I try as hard as I can to imbue the word with sarcasm, but actually I think it sounds like I'm just thanking him.

"So who's the lucky man?" he asks.

"Mitch Castellano."

I see him run down the football roster in his head. "I don't know that one."

"Basketball, I think."

"Ah."

"I don't really know him either."

"I'm sure you'll have fun," he says absently.

"Dad."

"Hmm?"

"I'm going to tell Dr. Landau the truth."

The look on his face changes. And it just kills me.

He knows what I'm talking about.

I wanted to be wrong about him. But I'm not. He may not know the details, but he knows there's something not right about the Prom Bowl. Maybe he's known all along. And he was going to ignore it.

"Ava, listen," he says, all serious-face.

I hold up a hand. "I don't want to listen. And I don't want to get into it. I'm not going to give you details because I want you to be able to say you didn't know about it. I want you to keep your job. But Dad, you should never have asked me to keep my mouth shut about this in the first place."

He draws back. "I never did that."

"You said not to spread rumors. And you didn't even listen to me. They weren't rumors. I knew *facts*. And when I told you I wanted out, you said I couldn't let you and Sean down. But you know what? You let *me* down."

"Ava, don't be melodramatic."

"I'm not being melodramatic. I'm being regular dramatic. My friend Solstice almost *died* at a party and I know what happened to her. That calls for drama."

He swipes a hand over his face, like he's trying to wipe away something invisible. "I wish you would let this go."

"Why, Dad? Why do you want me to do that?"

"Because it's not just about you and your friend."

"But it *is* about me. Plus, it's the right thing to do. Doesn't that even matter to you?"

"Of course it does, Ava." He doesn't meet my eyes.

"Just not as much as your football players?"

"What?"

"That's why you don't want me to tell." I feel numb. "It's not because you're afraid of being fired. It's because you're afraid the guys are going to get suspended."

"Honey, they have such bright futures. Especially Mark."

"But I don't have a bright future?" God, I sound shrill.

"I didn't say that."

"Sean says Mom wouldn't have let me do Prom Bowl. Do you think that's true?"

"She never had much appreciation for school spirit," he says.

"Is that why she left?"

Now he looks at me. His jaw is set, a muscle by his ear twitching, but otherwise he's expressionless. "What are you getting at?"

"Did Mom leave because she was sick of coming in second to football?"

"Watch it."

"What? Am I wrong? Or are you just mad because I'm saying it?"

"Whatever went on between us," he says, "it doesn't matter. She left, Ava. She made her choice."

"I want to see her," I say. "I want to go with Sean for spring break."

"No one ever said you couldn't visit her."

"Okay."

"Are you trying to punish me? Is that what this is? Is that why you're choosing now to go?"

"God, Dad, this isn't about you, okay?"

"I would never walk out on you," he says. "Nothing could ever make me abandon you or Sean. Nothing."

"What if it was us or coaching? What if you had to pick?"

"Why would I have to pick?"

"Oh my God, you can't do it." I feel like I'm watching this exchange from across the room. Like we're two strangers. "You wouldn't give up football for us."

"I didn't say that."

"But you didn't deny it."

"Ava, it's complicated. And you're giving me ridiculous ultimatums for no reason."

"It's not that complicated, actually. You're my dad. I love you. Stupid football obsession and all. I've always put you first. I've always chosen you. I chose you over my *mother*, Dad."

"Ava—"

"And I love Mom. Even though she left us. Which I'm still pissed at her for, but . . . she's Mom. I love her."

"She loves you too," he says. "You need to know that, Ava. You and Sean. She always loved you. She left me, not us. I should never have framed it that way."

He looks so upset, I almost want to let him off the hook. But I can't. I don't know if I can even trust what he's saying to me right now. "I'm still going to Dr. Landau first thing tomorrow morning."

"That's the wrong call, Ava."

"It's the call I'm making."

Silence. Total freeze-out.

"You need to back me up. You need to put me first. Ahead of football. Ahead of your career and your team and everything else. One damn time, Dad."

He shakes his head sadly, like I'm asking for the moon. Like I'm breaking his heart.

22

Mark

I've been up all night, and I'm not the all-nighter type. Cody is. Cody never studies for anything until the night before, and it's not like his grades are reprehensible. He just mainlines coffee for twelve straight hours leading up to exams and then is jacked all day. I don't even know how to make coffee, so I'm going to have to hit a convenience store on the way to school for a Monster energy drink.

That stuff will kill you, Ava would say, but the thing is, no, Ava, you'll kill me.

She's right that she has less to lose. Her record won't be scrutinized like mine is, and her dad can afford her education. She can take the hit of a suspension. I probably can't.

It's not like this was an easy call.

I tell myself that it's all right that this was hard for me.

Because in the end, I know—I am nearly, almost positive—that I'm making the right decision.

My parents are sitting up in bed sharing the newspaper. They're a couple of old romantics about newspapers. They divvy up the sections—Arts for Mom, Health and Science for Dad, World News and Sports shared between them. They clip out their favorite comic strips. They do the crossword together. Neither of them are due at work until noon—hooray for the restaurant industry—so they get to hang around and do this. Me, I have to go to the salt mines and act like I haven't just been awake for twenty-four hours straight.

Mom looks up. "Hey, there's my Fighting Irishman!"

"Fighting Irish," I correct her.

"Off to school early?"

"That's the spirit." Dad doesn't look up from his crossword. "Keep working hard in the home stretch."

The home stretch. It's the home stretch for all of us. My parents have been maybe-someday-ing my ear off since the day my pee-wee coach told them I had potential. I remember being nine years old, swimming in football gear designed for an adult frame and scaled down to child size. I remember my parents, in the front seat of the car we still have today, talking about doors opening, avoiding the word "college" as if saying it might jinx something. Before that summer, I was a bright kid whose parents cut him a lot of slack. After, every grade I brought home was examined and every subpar performance was noticed and commented on. They've invested almost ten years in getting me here. And I'm about to fuck it all up.

I'm definitely almost sure.

"I need to talk to you," I say.

"Sit," Dad says. "Solo in space."

"What?"

"Three letters," he holds up the crossword puzzle.

"Seriously? Han."

He slaps his forehead. "I thought it meant *alone* in space."

"That is why your son is going to Notre Dame and you are not, dear," Mom says.

My stomach churns. "About that."

"Is everything all right?" Mom asks.

Deep breath. "I'm going to be suspended today."

The pause is excruciating. If they cry, I'm going to fucking die on the spot.

"What does the school think you did?" Mom asks.

"What do you mean, suspended?" Dad says. "What does this mean for your scholarship?"

"Notre Dame can rescind it because of a suspension," I tell him.

"We'll go to Dr. Landau," Mom says. "Whatever the misunderstanding is, we'll straighten it out."

God, who wouldn't kill for that kind of innocent-until-proven-guilty presumption from their mother? "It's not a misunderstanding."

"What do you mean?"

"They've got grounds to suspend me. I'm turning myself in."

In this very moment, I see my mother's heart break. It's written on her face.

I see my dad's mind racing through a list of all the things I might have done. All the things kids are suspended for. Cheating on tests. Dealing drugs. Truancy. Sexual assault. It's a spectrum. It's minor crimes and major ones. Did I throw a freshman football player down a flight of stairs as part of a demented hazing ritual? Or did I smoke a cigarette out the window of a bathroom and get caught? I brace myself for the questions.

But they aren't asking.

They aren't going to absolve me.

Because to them, the worst possible thing I can do is destroy the family dream. That's rock bottom. Who cares how I did it?

Ava

Sean bails as soon as we get to school, out the door of Dad's car and down the steps to the lower-level entrance to the freshman wing. That door is also closest to the senior hallway, so ordinarily I'd be following him. But Dr. Landau's office is on the second floor, and today I'm going straight there.

I exit the car, expecting Dad to pull away to the faculty lot, but instead he puts it in park and gets out with me. "What's going on?"

"I'm going with you," he says.

"That wasn't the plan."

"C'mon, kid."

"Seriously, Dad. I don't want you losing your job over this."

"You let me worry about that," he says. "You're entitled to have a parent with you. You deserve that, Ava."

I swallow this like chicken soup, letting it warm me all the way down. "Thanks, Dad."

As soon as I pull open the door to the office, my heart drops.

Mark is here.

He's sitting in a chair, running his fingers over the glossy edges of a college pamphlet. I stop in my tracks and my dad walks straight into me. "Mark?"

He looks up at me and jumps to his feet. "Ava."

"Mr. Palmer," Dad rumbles.

"Coach Vanguard."

I pull away from Dad. "Mark, what are you doing here? I told you not to come."

In response, he grips my wrist and pulls me close, wraps me in a hug that is strong enough to block out where we are and what we're about to do. I hug him back, trying to memorize everything about this moment. The awkward way my nose smushes against his sternum, the boy smell that makes me want to pull him closer than is physically possible, the way he lifts me onto my tiptoes so I'm nearly hanging from his shoulders. *This is what it feels like to be loved,* I tell future-Ava. *Don't forget.*

Dad clears his throat.

I step back. "Mark, you should go."

"No, I shouldn't."

"No, you should. Sol and Cody were suspended. I am going to be suspended. If you don't get out of here—"

The inside office door opens. Dr. Landau sticks his head out. "Mr. Palmer? Ah, Greg! To what do I owe the pleasure?"

"I think we're all here for the same reason," Dad says.

"In that case, why don't you come in?"

Mark takes a seat on a hard bench facing Dr. Landau's desk. Dad selects a more comfortable-looking armchair. After a moment of hesitation, I sit between them on the bench. "Now then," Dr. Landau says, folding his hands, "what's this all about?"

I thought this was going to be excruciating, but I can't get the words out fast enough. I have to be the one to tell, before Mark can. "It's the Prom Bowl."

"The Prom Bowl? What about it?"

"The party that caused Solstice Downing to be hospitalized. It was a Prom Bowl event."

The principal shakes his head. "Nonsense. Prom Bowl is a school-sponsored function."

"It's true, sir," Mark speaks up.

"But the Prom Bowl events are competitive."

"It was a Girls Gone Wild party," I explain, and I swear I can feel my dad tense up next to me. "That's why Solstice was so drunk. It was a drinking contest."

"A Girls Gone Wild party. What else happens at such a party?"

I'm very, very conscious of my father sitting next to me. "We had to, um . . ."

"Perform challenges," Mark fills in.

"And what form did these challenges take? I assume it wasn't just drinking?"

"The girls could . . . they had the choice to take a drink or kiss someone or . . . " Mark's voice disappears into a mumble.

"What was that, Mr. Palmer?"

"Take something off."

"Clothes?"

"Yeah."

"In other words, our female students were compelled to become intoxicated and perform sexual acts."

"It wasn't—" I cut myself off. It *was* like that.

"I take it you knew about this, Greg?" Dr. Landau says.

"I just found out last night," Dad says.

"Are you sure? It seems two of your players were the ringleaders."

"The boys are under strict guidelines regarding alcohol," Dad says. "We have a zero-tolerance policy. Had I known anything like this was going on, the players involved would have lost their places on the team."

"Cody Spencer did lose his place on your team, didn't he?"

"Unrelated. That was performance-based. Mr. Palmer has been exemplary as a player, and I admire the fact that he is coming forward with this information now."

Hang on. Dad admires Mark for coming forward? Didn't he just this morning tell me that going to Dr. Landau was the wrong call?

Dr. Landau leans over the desk, which is the teacher version of getting all up in your face. "What about your daughter's involvement?"

Mark speaks up. "Ava's not to blame. The girls were manipulated."

"No," Dr. Landau says. "That's no excuse. Did anyone hold them down and pour liquor down their throats?"

"Well, no."

"Then they drank it willingly."

"It's not that simple."

"Zero tolerance," Dr. Landau says. "It *is* that simple. Underage drinking is grounds for suspension."

"I wasn't drinking," I say. "Just for the record. Neither was Mark."

"Ms. Vanguard, I'm sorry, but everyone knows you've been participating in the Prom Bowl. Your dedication has been a topic of conversation among the faculty all year. Everyone's been very impressed with the effort you've put forth, your school spirit, the drive that's taken you to the top of the pack."

What? "No, that was . . . I was never trying to—"

"You cannot expect me to believe that in the eleventh hour you decided this competition didn't matter to you anymore."

"She wasn't drinking," Mark says.

Dr. Landau shakes his head. "We can't just take the word of her boyfriend." He looks at Dad for backup.

"You know," Dad says, "she did break curfew that night."

"Dad!"

"Sorry, honey. Truth will out."

"But you didn't know what was going on with her involvement in the Prom Bowl?" Dr. Landau asks, eyebrow raised in clear disbelief.

"You know how teenagers are," Dad says, like they're old chums. Like he's talking about someone who isn't sitting right here, who isn't his own daughter. "Everything's a secret. Can't get the truth out of them."

Like I haven't been trying to hold the truth up to him for weeks now.

Dr. Landau nods. "Who else was involved in this?"

"Just me and Cody," Mark says.

"We'll have to speak to the other girls who were competitors in that round. Who was that? Catherine Pierce, right?"

I don't answer.

"This will go easier if you tell us," Dr. Landau says.

Maybe. I have no idea if he has any way of finding out who the top five girls were. He's got me and Sol. Maybe he can't get Kylie, Caity, and Charlotte. Maybe this is as far as it has to go.

"Was this the only party?" Dr. Landau asks. "Or have there been many?"

"Just this one," Mark says.

"Two weeks' suspension for each of you," Dr. Landau says. "Effective immediately."

It's what I expected, but I still feel like my insides are melting.

I've never been in trouble before, never even gotten detention. I look over at Dad, but he won't meet my eyes.

"That's unfair!" Mark's halfway off the bench, leaning across Dr. Landau's desk. "That's completely unreasonable."

"Mark," Dad says, "sit."

"Coach, you can't let him do this."

"Your behavior has consequences, Mr. Palmer," Dr. Landau says.

"I'm not talking about me," Mark says. "You can't do this to Ava."

"Mark," Dad says, "just settle down. You're not helping."

"Sir, she didn't do anything wrong. She was just *there.* She didn't organize the thing, she didn't drink. And now she's the one coming forward about what happened. What are you punishing her for?"

"Participation in this Girls Gone Wild party is against Patterson's code of conduct," says Dr. Landau.

"She was *recruited* for Prom Bowl. She was pushed into this at every turn. Blaming her is—is fucking *ridiculous.*"

"That's enough!" Dr. Landau snaps. His jaw is twitching.

Dad reaches over and tugs the back of Mark's shirt, dragging him back into his seat. For a minute my father's arm is around me. I want to lean against him and close my eyes, like I used to do when I was little.

He takes his arm back. "Will these suspensions be reported to their colleges of choice?"

I don't have a college of choice. I haven't made my choice yet. He's still not talking about me.

Dr. Landau presses his lips together. "We won't contact the schools, but we can't prevent them from requesting the students' records on their own."

Dad casts a worried glance at Mark, straight past me, and nods.

"One more thing," Dr. Landau adds. "This year's prom will be cancelled."

"For everybody?" I ask.

"Prom is a privilege," he says. "It must be earned. It's now my belief that by allowing our students to run the Prom Bowl, we've perpetuated the idea that the event belongs to them. Furthermore, I don't feel the students can be trusted with a high-profile party. So yes, Ms. Vanguard, the event will be cancelled for everyone. And I want a full list of the other participants by the end of the day. Dismissed."

Mark

"See me in my office after school," Coach Vanguard says.

"I . . . don't have school," I remind him. "We're suspended."

"Right. Of course." I can see he hasn't thought through the practicalities as they apply to this immediate week. "I have class. . . ."

"Ava," I say, "I can give you a ride."

I'm expecting her to look to her father for permission, but she takes my hand and starts toward the exit without a word.

"Should we talk to your dad?" I ask, following in her wake.

"No. The hell with him."

"He showed up for you, at least."

"He showed up for *you*. He just wanted to make sure you wouldn't lose your scholarship. He completely threw me under the bus."

"I'm sure he didn't mean to—"

"Stop defending him, Mark." She shoves the door so hard it bangs against the side of the building. "He only cares about me as long as I'm being a *team player*."

I pull her around to face me. "Hey. Stop."

"Why?"

"I care."

"I told you not to come today, Mark. Why did you do that?"

"Because I couldn't let you take the fall for me. I couldn't be that guy."

"Well, it didn't work. I still got suspended. And now you might lose your scholarship."

"It's okay."

"*How* is it okay?"

"Well—fine, it's not okay. Fuck. I mean, yeah, I probably just threw my life away, shit . . ." Breathe. Keep it steady. "But I had to, Ava."

"Is this some kind of weird winning me back thing? Because I'm not fucking worth that, Mark."

"We're not going to talk about what you're *worth* anymore. Fuck that. And no. I'm not trying to win you back. Fuck winning you, too."

Her eyes are wet. She's going to cry, and she's still pissed off. I love this girl. I love her. "Then why?" she asks.

"Because I had a hand in all this and I had to take responsibility."

"It's on me too," she says. "Next time someone tells me I have to do something fucked up, I'll tell them where to get off."

"What if I tell you that you have to come get nachos at Sonny's with me?"

"Go to hell," she grins.

"Okay, well, what if I *ask* you to come with me?"

"Hot dog too," she counters.

"Done."

23

Ava

Bottom line—I have to get out of this town.

I can't face anyone here anymore. No one except Mark and Sean has spoken to me since prom was cancelled. And even with Mark, it's a little awkward. Notre Dame got word of the suspension and rescinded their scholarship offer. He's going to Baylor now, which is a perfectly decent school for both football and academics, but it's also way down in Texas. That makes it even harder to entertain the idea of a long-distance relationship. And with all the time I've had to myself, I've had plenty of opportunities to slip into fantasies about how nice it would be if we were still together.

Tonight would have been prom night, and I can't help wondering what it would have been like if the Prom Bowl had never happened. My senior prom. I would have gotten ready at Charlotte's, I think, because she wouldn't hate me, and maybe Kylie and some of their other friends would have been there too. Aunt Claire would have done our hair and we'd have helped each other with makeup. We'd have exclaimed over each other's dresses and teased each other about our dates.

Instead of taking pictures of me like a proud parent, Dad's at a school board hearing for faculty members under suspicion of complicity in the Prom Bowl. He might get fired. And consequently, he's really not speaking to me either. It's less blatant than it is at school—he doesn't sneer when he sees me or anything—but it's also so much worse.

It's like Sean said. No matter what, he's still Dad.

The only person who's still completely normal with me, the only person whose life I haven't ruined, is Sean, and he's been at the arcade for the past hour and a half because he still has friends in this town.

Talk about being alone on prom night.

The third episode of my *Love It or List It* marathon starts, and I crack open my second can of Coke. Brenda and Tom are reluctant to leave their crappy old house, and the realtor is trying to sell them on a much nicer one that's in the suburbs instead of the middle of the woods. Brenda and Tom are hesitant. I feel that. I'd go live in the middle of the woods if I could. Wouldn't it be something to get up every morning knowing you wouldn't have to see another human being all day?

This is the kind of thinking Dad hates. But on the other hand, if I'd stayed home and minded my business all year, none of this would have happened.

It's strange to admit this, but I don't know what anyone does for fun around here when they're *not* auctioning themselves off to the highest bidder. Where will all the other kids be tonight, since they're not at prom? It's hard to believe everyone's just sitting at home watching reality TV. What is there to do in this town? Sonny's? The movie theater?

No, it's Friday night, and they're probably at a party. That's the difference all this has made. Everyone's still probably hanging out, just without me.

And apparently I *want* to be at a party with my classmates, so that's weird.

No.

No, that isn't what I want, is it.

God, Ava, you poor fucking cliché.

This is about a boy.

This is stupid. Mark and I are friends. These days, he's the only friend I've got. We're graduating in two weeks and he's going to Texas and I'm going to California and we need to let this be what it is. It's the right thing. It's the responsible thing.

I check my phone. Nada. Obviously. No one's going to text me. I deleted my Facebook app after three straight days of hate messages following the news of prom being cancelled. I'm sure they're still accumulating somewhere in the cloud, since I never got rid of my account, but I'm not going to look at them. I have just about enough willpower for that.

The doorbell rings.

During my suspension, some idiot tried to pull the old have-a-pizza-sent-to-the-wrong-address prank, which is apparently a thing people do in real life. The joke was on the prankster though, because pizza is delicious and I was more than willing to pay. I think they must have known someone working at the pizza place, though, because the pie had the word "bitch" spelled out in olives. As if I'm that easy to scare. I don't know who's at the door tonight, but I'm sort of hoping for something like that. I've got a twenty I wouldn't mind dropping on a meal from the mayor of bittertown, or whoever sends these yummy hate-grams.

I see him through the beveled glass of the front door before I open it, though, and I know this isn't pizza. And yet, as I'm wrestling with the sticky deadbolt, I'm still trying to make the warped image resolve into the figure of a delivery boy.

I get the door open. Finally.

And there he is. As if I'd ordered him.

"Hey, Ava."

"Why are you in a tux?" I blurt.

Mark grins. "That's a fine hello."

"You know prom's cancelled, right? Oh God, it's not back on, is it?"

"You don't think you'd have heard if prom was back on?"

"I think if that happened, everyone would incredibly prefer it if I didn't show up."

"Prom's not back on."

"Then what? Wedding? Funeral?"

"Weirdo."

"Bar mitzvah?"

He brings a hand out from behind his back. He's holding a

small box, about the size of a cupcake. "Will you be my date?"

"Your date to what?" Oh God, there's a corsage in that box. "Mark."

He opens the box and pulls out the flowers. "It's not for prom."

"You're wearing a tux. You bought a corsage."

"Go get dressed."

"I don't have a dress."

"Wear that thing you wore to the fashion show. That was pretty."

"That wasn't mine. Mark, where are we even going?"

"Sonny's, I thought. And then the park. Some kids are meeting up there."

"They hate me."

"Nah. It's kind of an anti-prom thing. You should be there."

"I'm just the girl who came in senior year and ruined everyone's prom."

"No," he says, "that isn't all you are."

He takes my hand, and before I know it, the band of the corsage is sliding over my wrist. I raise it to my face and inhale. It's white roses, tiny ones, the buds hardly open, and the smell is earthy and impossibly rich. "It's okay if you don't have a dress," he says. "Wear whatever. Wear this."

"My Cookie Monster pajamas?"

"Whatever you want."

"Hang on," I tell him. "Just give me five minutes."

• • •

The big lesson of moving, I think, is that you don't really need all your stuff. We've been here for nearly a year and I still have unopened boxes in the recesses of my closet. It's crap, mostly—old laptops and phones that broke or got upgraded, books from childhood that I never got rid of, a ratty old cloth tote bag I don't use anymore, all my souvenirs from our family trips to Disney World and Wisconsin Dells and Hannibal, Missouri.

And neatly folded at the bottom of one box—a barely worn yellow dress. A gift from my mother, who I'm learning to forgive.

It still fits.

Mark

"Are you excited about Baylor?" Ava asks.

I take a fry from the tray she's holding out. It's soggy with the weight of cheese, sour cream, chives, and bacon, and my fingers are instantly coated. Sonny does not skimp on the condiments, particularly in to-go orders. "You know what? I think you're the first person who's asked me that."

"You're kidding."

"I mean, the Baylor people might have said something."

"But not your friends? Your parents? *My* dad?"

"All too focused on the great tragedy of my scholarship—*pfft*."

"Ugh."

"It's like death at my house. My mom can't even look at me."

"My dad too. He's really disappointed."

"*I'm* really disappointed."

"I'm so sorry. About Notre Dame."

"No, not about that." I take another fry. "I just feel like . . . we should have done better, you know? We shouldn't have let things go as far as they did."

"I just keep thinking Sean won't have to do it," she says. "He can like girls and ask them out, and go to prom and to parties if he wants, without any of the bullshit."

"That's a bonus."

"No," she says. "That's everything."

Mitch Castellano walks over from the other side of the park and hands me a couple of beers. "Bogarting my girl, Palmer?"

"*Your* girl?" I challenge him as Ava stiffens next to me.

"I won her," Mitch says, "fair and square." He turns to Ava. "Plenty of room on my blanket, babe."

"I'll bet there is," she says dryly.

Mitch laughs uncertainly, like he's not sure whether he's the joke, and wanders off.

I hand Ava one of the beers. "Well played."

"Thirteen people at this party and one of them had to be that guy."

"Decent group otherwise, though," I say. Most of the others are clustered around the fire pit. Denise Mellibosky and Zoe West are inseparable, cuddling and passing around ingredients for s'mores, occasionally kissing. Caity Pierce is rounding second base with some guy from the basketball team. "I'm surprised how many of the Prom Bowl girls showed up."

"Well, we never like to miss a party," says a voice from behind.

I turn. "Hey Solstice!"

Ava jumps up and hugs her, and Solstice hugs back. "Sol! You're free?"

"My parents are going to breathalyze me when I get home," she rolls her eyes. "But I managed to convince them that prom was too big a milestone to miss out on, even if it is cancelled."

"Damn straight." I knock my beer against her imaginary drink.

"Your new school doesn't have a prom?" Ava asks.

"Eh. Who wants to go to prom with a bunch of strangers?"

Ava looks thoughtful.

"You wishing you were in Carbondale?" I ask her.

She shakes her head. "My real friends are here."

Solstice knocks her shoulder against Ava's. "I'm gonna go see about those s'mores. Coming?"

"In a few."

"So," I say as Solstice runs off. "UCLA?"

"Yeah."

"You have a major picked out?"

She laughs.

"What?"

"This is how we met. You'd think we'd have come up with something better to talk about by now."

"You'd think! And yes."

"What?"

"Yes, I'm excited about Baylor. And I don't want to spend tonight apologizing to each other."

"Easy for you to say," she says.

"Hey. I did some shit. But I just want to get out of here, you know? Forget about all this."

She shakes her head and takes a long drink of her beer, throwing her head back to expose her long neck. "That would be a mistake," she says at last.

"You think?"

"I think we need to remember what happened here. How bad it got. I think it changed us. And I'll be damned if I'm gonna go off to college and let something like this happen all over again."

"Pretty sure they don't have Prom Bowls in college," I say.

"I don't mean that. I'm talking about proving that I'm worth someone's time and attention. I don't have to do that. I shouldn't waste my time with that."

I nod, getting it. "And nobody should ever ask you to."

Micah Foster cuts off our conversation with a shout as one of his bottle rockets takes to the sky. The kids around the park break away from what they're doing, from their conversations and kisses and cans of cheap beer, to watch. Micah is, I think, here with Kylie Richards, who's standing close to his side and wearing a leather jacket over her prom dress. She expertly sets up the next bottle rocket as I watch.

"Are we going to get in trouble for this?" Ava asks.

"Probably not. I doubt Micah has a permit, but no one would know that unless they came checking. And honestly, on prom night? Cops have bigger problems."

Another bottle rocket goes off. From across the expanse of the park, I can hear Solstice cheering.

Ava leans over and kisses me.

She catches me up in the familiar—the mess of her hair, the fruity smell that's probably shampoo but might just be *her*, the way she moves her tongue against mine (which she learned from me). And yeah, she is the best high school girlfriend I could have hoped for, but—

"I thought you said we were over," I say, unwilling to draw back from her in case it breaks the spell, my lips moving right against hers as I speak.

"I say a lot of things," she says into my mouth. "I can change my mind if I want. Wild Card, remember?"

She wraps her arms around me and pulls me down onto the blanket. The fireworks continue above us, probably, but I'm not paying attention anymore.

ACKNOWLEDGMENTS

This is probably the closest I'll ever get to giving an Oscar acceptance speech, so I'd better not waste it. Okay. Here goes: To my editor, Catherine Laudone—I have so thoroughly enjoyed building stuff in this sandbox. This book would not even remotely exist without you, and I can't thank you enough for the opportunity and all the fun. Further thanks are due to the rest of the BFYR team for everything from cover art to comma placement. Working with you is a genuine privilege.

My agent, John Cusick, sees things in my books that I didn't know were there. He may think I'm much smarter than I really am, and we must hope he never finds me out. In the meantime, I couldn't imagine a better human to have in my corner.

Alanah, who eagerly takes on the work of reading my early drafts, is to thank for the shoring up of many plot holes. You make me feel like a real live writer.

Hannah—you're the main reason I get to do this at all, you know. Thanks for the boost. You make me a better feminist, and this story would suck without you.

Thanks to The Four of Us—Teri, who made me believe I could write books; Leah, who taught me everything I know about football and Minnesota; and Sarah, who gets stories to the people who need them. Additional thanks to my amateur publicist, Liza, for going the extra miles.

ACKNOWLEDGMENTS

To Maria, who has always read my writing, including my terrible *Star Wars* crossover fanfiction from when I was fifteen, and who consistently provides the most convincingly positive feedback.

And to Jeff, who makes me promise not to give up.